ALL BUSINESS IS THEIR PLEASURE

THREE EROTIC WOMEN STORYLINES

HEATHER STOLTZ

plicit Press

REAL ESTATE MOGUL

It doesn't take much to convince Vivian to hire Bradley. He has impeccable organizational twenty-seven-year-old skills and received gleaming recommendations from all three of his previous employers, who had all been sad to see the twenty-seven-year-old go, but who were not going to stand in the way of his progress.

This is the busiest time of year for Vivian. Her company, StarStruck Realty, handles the bulk of Texas's real estate, and so she needs an assistant, fast. The previous one has just left in a halo of French terms that included a bevy of *'fuck yous'* and the odd *'you fucking psycho bitch'* being hurled from the demure Jehovah's Witness at a cool, calm, and collected Vivian.

Vivian is known for her taste for unavailable cock. She can't help herself. A powerful woman, she knows she can have any dick she wants. But she wants unavailable cock, this desire compounded it seems by the fact that she herself is unavailable.

Anyway, she managed to find herself impaled by a certain Puerto Rican a few days before Lana stormed in to her office and hurled profanities along with her resignation at her. Not entirely unknown to Vivian, the 12-inch Puerto Rican dick that had impaled her *was attached to Lana's husband!*

So now Bradley, who's pretty much aced the interview so far, is sitting across from her and waiting for her to confirm as much. Vivian throws her eyes to the knob on her door. It's in the locked position. She had asked him to lock it because the door didn't catch properly and would swing open constantly. This is a lie.

Vivian gives the stocky young man the once over again before getting up and instructing him to sit in her chair. A little confused, Bradley does what he's told.

"Now you interview me!"

"Excuse me, ma'am?"

"You heard me Bradley; interview me for your position."

Vivian assumes a huskier tone that immediately makes Bradley warmer under the collar. He stumbles through a few questions that make it clear that while he knows a lot about StarStruck Realty, he definitely isn't the boss. Vivian answers shyly and makes a valiant attempt at being awkward and vulnerable, a move that immediately sees Bradley become more assertive, more authoritative, and more like the boss.

She commends him, breathing heavy enough to be heard and hard enough for her breasts to dance up and down on her chest. Bradley can't take his eyes off the ebony goddess's mounds. He follows her breasts as she stands up and then comes around to her side of the desk again. She leans her voluptuous ass against the side of the table and allows her skirt to ride up her thighs without correcting it. Bradley's eyes are already on her legs.

She lets him sit a minute longer and then instructs him with her eyes to vacate her seat. She knows he can't. Not now. His cock has filled his pants and rests erect across his thigh. It's a massive rod. Vivian wants it. But she can't be the one to ask for it. He needs to initiate. Her cunt is beating hard between her legs and she really hopes that he makes this request quickly.

He too breathes heavily now. He looks up and down the length of her legs. He knows that this is probably going to mean the end of the interview, and his prospects at Star-Struck, but he just can't help himself.

"Oh fuck it!" he says finally.

He moves off the chair and gets onto his knees in front of Vivian. Lifting her skirt he pulls down her panties without waiting for her permission. Bradley is a man possessed now and nothing in the room exists except the beautiful blackberry in front of him.

"I'm a married woman..." Vivian manages.

"I know. I'm sorry..." Bradley breathes.

She knows that all she has to do is say no, or push his head off her cunt. She can't. This is exactly what she wants. She can only hope now that the man whose tongue is spitting fire into her vagina will not be an awkward mess afterward who runs screaming from the building, never to be heard from again.

Bradley lodges his thick tongue deep inside Vivian pleased that she starts almost immediately pissing the contents of her pussy into his mouth. Vivian continues to feed him her juices while he pulls hard on her clit and then fucks her harder with his tongue. He starts to undo his pants and again she hopes that the build-up has not been in vain and that the young man now fumbling in his wallet for a condom doesn't have a sudden attack of conscience.

He doesn't, and without looking at her he eases his dick inside her. Vivian braces herself on his shoulders and proceeds to take every inch of him into her. He fucks her like a man on death row eating his last meal, savoring every bite. Deep, patient strokes belie his youth and in a steady, consistent movement Bradley brings Vivian to one of the absolute best fucking orgasms she's had in years.

"You've got the job," she stutters as he cleans the absolute gusher she's sprayed all over him. It takes him a good twenty minutes under the hand-drier in the men's room to get himself in a state to leave the building without looking like he's just had a shower with his pants on...

It takes less than a week for Bradley to establish himself as Vivian's plus-one. Even while she screams at everyone around her, he moves calmly through the office, dealing not just with her admin, but also with his own real estate clients. He has proven to be better than even his credentials had suggested.

To everyone who isn't Bradley, Vivian Washington isn't just a real estate mogul, she is a dictator extraordinaire. Profanities filter out of her office as easily and regularly as property deals filter in. Everyone accepts this as normal soon enough; just a typical day in the world that is Vivian Washington's.

Vivian is truly one of the most successful black women in the state. Heading up StarStruck Realty, in Texas no less, is in itself no easy feat. And to be black in Texas, the same state that took Oprah to task over their cattle industry, it took balls to set up shop here.

But she has, and now her clientele reads like a list of the who's who of Cattle Country, the biggest names in town, all eager to do business with her. She has the gift of the gab and looks that make her way with words lethal. Despite her obvious charm though, Vivian isn't above using underhanded tactics to close a deal. Every war has its casualties after all, and real estate is a bloody battlefield on the best of days.

When she isn't ruling the property world, Vivian is wife to Randy Hall, a former basketball standout from the University of Texas – Highland Park. They married in an elaborate ceremony, a $50,000 fairy-tale paid for by Vivian as a reward for the life she never had back in Indianapolis. Her wedding was her gift to the little girl inside herself that never had much back then.

Fortunately, Randy has managed to build a successful construction company and has since lavished his wife with several gifts exceeding the price of their wedding and therefore has reclaimed his manhood. But reclaiming this title hasn't done much for their sex life, the best sex, and also the most memorable, being the first time Randy Hall fucked her. It's been downhill ever since.

Randy Hall is a tall man, and the first time Vivian had given in to his sexual advances, four dates into their relationship, she expected that he would have a big cock. But what she hadn't expected was fifteen inches of thick dick. Even with her experience and her youth, the fifteen inches was more than she bargained for.

They had had a romantic dinner on the floor of Randy's college apartment, and with two glasses of red in her, she knew that a third would be all that was needed for her legs to relax as much as her heart. She was right. Wine, particularly red wine, had a way of working through every part of Vivian's body and makes her a whole lot more receptive to dick.

Randy helped her out of her clothes and then let her watch him undress. He let her touch his cock and run her fingers over the full length of it, acquainting herself with its massiveness. She fondled his balls, sending his dick into full mast each time her hands cupped the large nuts. Vivian then made a valiant attempt at sucking what was clearly too much cock for her pretty little mouth.

There was no point in prolonging her agony and so Randy laid the petite Vivian on the ground. He met her cunt with his full lips while his hands found her breasts. Vivian pulled her legs up over his shoulders and let them run down his back. She pushed down onto him as his tongue drove into her. Her first orgasm came in minutes. Randy was pleased at the excessive wetness shooting out of her vagina because it meant his cock wouldn't be met by a hostile environment.

Randy could never find condoms that fit his enormous cock, but Vivian had already been on contraception for a while. So he fed her his massive head, clean and uncovered. He stretched her pussy wider than she had ever thought possible and less than an inch after his tip made full entry she was gasping for him to stop. He came down to her mouth with his instead, driving a further five inches into her by the time they were kissing.

His kissing was as intense as his cock, and Vivian shifted focus repeatedly between the two. By the time Randy was ramming his rod steadily in and out of her super-stretched cunt she had lost herself completely to him, and despite the size of his dick, Randy spent four solid hours bringing her repeatedly to the gentlest orgasms she has ever had in her life. He himself only shot his load once he was sure that she couldn't possibly go for another round.

Vivian brings herself from her memories of the fantastic fuck Randy once was as the sound of Bradley over the intercom filters into the restroom cubicle she's in and through her head. She really covers all her bases and no matter what you happen to be doing or where you are, you will not be able to escape Vivian.

"Meeting in thirty minutes... Conference Room B!" Bradley has already assumed Vivian's bark when he addresses the other agents.

"About what now..." Stanley asks.

Bradley shrugs off the question, knowing as does Stanley that the 'what' of Vivian's meetings is irrelevant. If she wants everyone in Conference Room B, then that is exactly where everyone is going to be no matter what it is they happen to be doing. After he is sure that the announcement has been received by everyone, Bradley heads toward Vivian's office.

She's not at her Cherry Wood desk when he enters the room, so he takes his usual look around. The art in the room still takes him aback and in Vivian's absence, he can give the pieces a relaxed review. This woman really does have exquisite taste.

The sculptures are by a number of artists from across the globe, but all her paintings are Van Gogh, prints mostly but still; Vivian had said on the day she interviewed him that Van Gogh was the only artist whose paintings didn't make her head hurt, something Bradley had always thought was odd given Van Gogh's mental history.

"Bradley!" The sound of her voice brings him from his revelry. She turns the knob, locking the door, and then walks toward him. "Good morning..." She's on him before he can reply.

He tries to keep a straight face despite his cock already bulging in his tight pants. "Yes ma'am, uhm, good...morning... always." His familiarity now with Vivian's fiery hot vagina makes him stutter. He knows that this will last no more than fifteen minutes, the same fifteen minutes it's lasted every morning for a week already, but it's the best fucking fifteen minutes of his day.

After Bradley's first interview, and his immediate employment, this special appointment, exclusively hers and his, was set up for every morning, just before they started calling clients or holding meetings. It sets the perfect tone for the rest of her day, as it did the day she first introduced herself to Bradley's cock. She's been quite content to have her regular fix of his dick every day since, and Bradley himself is yet to complain.

"Get on the desk!" His command is stern. She loves it, the authority in his voice wetting her cunt. Like a good little girl she obeys and mounts the desk.

"What type of panties are you wearing?" Bradley asks this while sending his hand under her skirt to feel for himself. Thankfully he finds nothing there but warm, wet cunt. He carefully unzips her skirt at the sides and pulls it down off her, placing it neatly on the far end of the table.

He parts her legs and slides her towards him. She falls back onto the table and before she can come back up he has stuck a finger inside her pussy. His other hand unzips his pants and whips out his cock. Bradley also wears no underwear, but for obvious reasons, all his pants are a very dark shade of gray. There's never a need to warm Vivian up so he always just comes prepared.

Bradley pulls his finger from her and slides her down towards his dick. He sends it into her just as soon as he has the condom on. She arches back so that he can only reach her neck. He loves to kiss, but Vivian finds it inappropriate. She moans deeply, her fingers white as they dig into the table. Bradley's fucking this morning is brazen, lacking the usual licks that send her over the edge. But time isn't on their side, as usual, Bradley having announced the meeting too soon.

He fucks her so hard that his hipbones collide with hers. His cock is so thick inside her that it bangs against her hardened clit, dragging it into Vivian's vagina almost. She jumps back onto the table in total ecstasy, but she catches the grand timepiece on the wall and pushes closer to him so that he hits her spot instantly. This is fucking awesome, but it also needs to be fucking quick.

Vivian closes her eyes, imagining Bradley pulling on her cunt lips and sucking on her clit as he'd done every day this week. She absolutely loves the feeling of his tongue flicking over her cunt. It is this thought now, this image of his mouth, warm on her cunt, fusing with the warmth of her pussy that makes for just the right fantasy to push her swiftly to the end.

He grabs the sides of her legs and pushes them together so that they sandwich his cock. His massive cock pulls the inside of Vivian's experienced pussy towards the entrance. They are both remarkably close and Vivian starts to make more noise than she would have liked. She mentions his name a few times, biting on her tongue each time she does because this is for her the ultimate vulnerability. She tightens her pussy to speed things up, her head suddenly on business.

Bradley gets her shirt undone and her bra off while distracting her with massive thrusts deep inside her. Her nipples are suddenly on the inside of his mouth and for a moment Conference Room B and even her vulnerability that saw her say his name in response to his dick's perfect technique are completely forgotten.

Bradley and everyone who's had the pleasure of pleasuring Vivian has dubbed her 'Splash'. The reason for this is seconds from affirming itself and Bradley knows it. He knows that he will never cum before Vivian now, her climax and the moments preceding it always very vocal. He slips his cock out of her as he descends to the ground and covers her hole with his mouth. He's just landed on her cunt, his tongue barely two licks in, when she lets out a loud, pleasure-filled scream and sprays a piss-load of cum down Bradley's throat.

Her juices fill his mouth, flow down his chin, and a little spray onto his clothes. Luckily, he has a clean shirt in his office. He will mumble some bullshit about spilled coffee and make his way to the washroom before the meeting. But before he makes his way out of the office there is the small matter of his large dick.

He's back on his feet again, his cock inside Vivian, thrusting madly as he darts to the end in less than two minutes. She's a creamer, a squirter, a waterfall, and in the two minutes to Bradley's climax, she squirts an unexpected second load. Fortunately, it shoots out of her only after Bradley has removed his cock and managed to duck out of the way.

Before dismissing him Vivian makes a dry joke about wanting him to provide the same service for someone else, saying that he would do it if he wanted to keep his job. She is surprised when he turns around and offers to quit, saying that he just wouldn't do it. His tone is firm again, his voice raised. This wets her cunt, but they do have a meeting to get to.

Refreshed and pulled together, they meet everyone in the conference room. Bradley is still a little bothered by Vivian's closing comments, not being one who cares too much for games. He hopes that it really was just a joke, but also determines that if it wasn't, he would not stand for it. He's only been here eight days but he's shown that he's a valuable employee. He just also happens to enjoy fucking the boss. The last thing he's going to do now is have his cock pimped off to secure additional business for StarStruck!

Vivian gets straight into it, Christina, Selene, Travis, and Stanley already seated at their usual spots at the large boardroom table.

"Christina, you need to start building a new portfolio of properties to show the Dallas Cowboys, Bradley, and the Texas Rangers are happy so far so keep it up. Stanley, you have a special request from the former state governor, I've emailed the details to you. And Selene, there's a new client on my desk that I want to discuss with you after I've looked at the file a bit more. So far the numbers look good for this quarter, and except for Travis who's got vacation time coming up, it's a full platoon for the silly season... Okay. Before we get started, does anyone have any questions?"

Christina speaks up. "I thought the Cowboys were done with us?"

Vivian smiles, "Leave them to me. I've got a meeting with John Lionel later. He'll come around!" Everyone in the room has some idea about what this means but they wouldn't dare say it. Bradley is visibly pissed off. He remains pissed off for the remainder of the day.

After wrapping up all the items on her schedule that required her to be at the office Vivian makes for the spa. It takes her a full day of treatments to be confident enough for her meeting with John. Not that she needs much done, being so well kept, but the psychology of it all requires the effort.

She arrives at John's house just after seven.

John receives her himself, opening the large door to a

woman who looks like she's slept her whole life in the arms of a God whose divine duty it was to keep her beautiful.

"Good evening Vivian. Welcome..."

It's an impressive residence, both inside and out. She makes sure to compliment him on his impeccable taste, and also points out that not only did she help him find this gem, but it was also her construction contacts that had helped with the renovations. Some of the art on the walls was also bought following referrals from her to some of her art people. By the time they sit down to dinner John Lionel has no doubt who he has to thank for the state of the home he now lives in.

John announces the menu with the arrogance of someone who knows exactly what he wants and the certainty of someone who always gets it. His chef has prepared stuffed chicken Marsala with a baked potato and asparagus shoots. And for dessert, they would be having key lime pie. John pours himself a glass of red wine, and Vivian, herself not much of a drinker anymore, compliments him on the bottle. She is aware of its quality. The bottled water she drinks is also of the highest quality.

They sit down to dinner and discuss everything but the business at hand. Vivian knows from experience that it is best to save the serious stuff for after dinner when the client is full and tipsy. There is also a thick sexual tension that hangs between them and the best time to play on that would be once she is close enough to him for him to smell her perfume and want to reach out and touch her. Dinner ends without incident, filled with talk of stats and teams and the state of football in general. Vivian's knowledge of the game hardens John's cock considerably.

"It's Christina," John says at last when they've finished

with dessert and are seated on the large settee by the fire in his massive living room.

Vivian looks confused. "I'm sorry?"

"Basically, we're looking for someone who is outgoing, fun, and aggressive. She's not it. She comes across as very nonchalant. And if she's not sure of the property that she's trying to sell us, then we're not comfortable buying it. A lot of these footballers are young, first-time buyers you know, and they need someone who is going to guide them through the process." John speaks candidly.

Vivian understands. She knows that Christina's laid-back style makes her seem, to some clients, uninterested in making the sale. But Vivian knows that this is because she is accustomed to dealing with clients who know exactly what they want and who simply need to be guided to the right properties and then left to make up their own minds. She isn't used to dealing with amateurs who need babysitting.

"Would it make a difference if I spoke to her, or assigned your portfolio to someone else in the office?"

"Would this someone else be like you?" John flirts openly.

"Come now John, no one is like me. But the person I have in mind does come a close second. She also has an excellent all-round taste and a great eye for choosing hous-es." There is of course no such person.

"As hot as you too I hope," John continues to flirt.

"Hardly, Christina is the hottest female next to me in the office, also the only available one if one of your boys got lucky. But if it's aggression you want, then I've got the perfect mother-hen to guide your little puppies on their journey through the big bad world of buying property." Vivian knows what she's doing, not wanting to lose this client for Christina, who has done a stellar job up until now and really is a profit-turner.

"In that case, have a chat with Christina; put some fire in the girl. The last thing I need is to burden stressed footballers with an ugly battle-ax."

They both laugh as it becomes clear that John, and probably his team, just want someone beddable in case it happened.

Vivian studies his face for a minute before getting up. "Well then, I should get going." She puts her virgin *cosmo* on the side table and waits for John to get up and escort her to the door. He doesn't move, the biggest grin on his face.

"I take it then that I'll be showing myself out?" Vivian wonders where the gentleman who had pulled her chair for her earlier has disappeared to.

"I'd love to get up Ms' Washington, but I'm afraid that the smell of your perfume has had an unexpected effect on my cock, and should I move, you would be privy to a sight that might offend you."

"I'm not easily offended Mr. Lionel, but I do have to get home to my husband. It is MRS WASHINGTON as you well know..." It actually isn't, Vivian having kept her maiden name for business reasons. Her husband is Randy Hall.

"Well ain't MR WASHINGTON just the luckiest bastard in Texas!"

Vivian laughs. "He probably is. I really must go."

She shows herself out, not wanting the temptation of his cock, despite its availability. John Lionel isn't married. Or even in a relationship. She thinks. Vivian didn't mess with athletes, and only rarely with clients. She knows that John isn't used to getting turned down but since she's managed to get him back in her game, there was no need to pull out the big guns. She would just have to give Christina a crash course in aggression and a heads up on the real reason John Lionel wants a hot realtor. It is flattering though that he finds her most attractive, but Vivian is genuinely not interested in anything but his team's business.

She leaves John wanting her more than he had when she arrived...

Vivian has an urgent meeting with Christina the next morning. By the time she leaves Vivian's office, they've discussed strategy and set up a series of appointments that will see her transformed overnight into a sultry, fiery, twenty-two-year-old white version of Vivian. That should keep John Lionel and his players happy.

Alone in her office, Vivian peruses a folder on her desk. A new corporation is expanding into Austin and they need accommodation for their executives. It's always best to let a woman handle high-powered Caucasian executives, and the only available woman in the office at the moment is Selene. Now Selene isn't the brightest button on the blazer, but she is sufficiently attractive. And Vivian does owe her. Not that Selene knows this of course. Vivian summons her into her office to discuss this new business, her guilt overriding her business sense momentarily.

Waiting for Selene to arrive, Vivian remembers why...

━━

Selene's fiancé had come into the office to surprise her at the end of her first week at StarStruck. It was lunchtime and there was nobody at the front desk, so Vivian had received him. Selene was out in the field and Vivian had told Tom, Selene's fiancé, as much. He said he would come back later but she offered him the comfort of the staff lounge to wait. They didn't want to call her and ruin the surprise.

Tom had the attractiveness and sex appeal of a very handsome nerd. Having missed her regular appointment with Bradley, who was home with the flu, Vivian had been dripping all morning, her pussy desperate for dick. So now, she practically paraded herself in front of the man who sat on the largest sofa in the room, twitching nervously.

His lanky frame was supported by broad shoulders and exaggerated biceps. There was something about geeks that had them over-commit to the gym. Tom was tall, almost slender, and if there was one thing Vivian knew about men of this build, it was that they, like her husband, usually had massive cocks. So she had to at least try to take advantage of this opportunity.

Vivian's beauty was entrancing. At 5'3", the color of chocolate, with big brown eyes framed by long, well-kept hair, she was way more attractive than Selene. Selene had just enough ass, where Vivian had plenty, and boobs to match. She knew that it would not be too difficult to persuade this man to fuck her if he was inclined to explore cunt that wasn't Selene's.

There is a moment in any situation where you just know how it's going to go. That moment came quickly for Vivian and Tom. It could have been because there was nobody else around. Lunchtime was the only time each day when the only person at StarStruck was the boss. She loved this time, to breathe, catch up, and fit in a fuck. The *fuck* had walked in totally unexpected, but here it was.

Tom's biceps strained under his shirt, too big for the size of the fabric covering them. His arms were probably this geek's attempt to affirm their masculinity. Whatever the reasons, they didn't matter. What mattered most at that moment was that he whips out some serious dick and does some serious fucking.

Vivian lets his hand sit on hers longer than needed when she hands him the coffee she made herself. The electricity moves through her from him like a static shock. It literally is her shoes on the carpet doing what science demands. They laugh as the cup is almost dropped, and at the fact that despite the charge Tom's fingers stayed put.

The cup is put down as words become unnecessary, the wall clock giving them just under half an hour to attend to this temptation before the office is abuzz again. They make for the privacy of Vivian's office with the *reliable* lock on the door.

Tom immediately turns Vivian over and takes from her any control she thought she would have in this situation. He lifts her skirt above her perfect bubble butt and smiles at the absence of underwear. She wants to turn around, to see the cock she's about to get, but he holds her down hard and tells her to brace herself.

She smiles...

His teeth sink deep into her ass cheeks repeatedly. He bites into the soft, yet firm flesh over and over again as he works her legs apart, feeling all the way up and down the strong thick legs that both end in eight-inch heels. Vivian moans once his tongue is in her crack and then digging out her ass. A moment later it's on her vagina, wetting her snatch rather efficiently.

Tom sends a finger so thick into her cunt that for a second she assumes that it's his cock. He feeds her a second, letting her know that only once she can take four of his fingers inside her will she be ready for his dick. She giggles audibly, unintentionally so and this has Tom confirm what he is saying by pulling out his cock and running it between her butt-cheeks. He thrusts all the way up and then all the way down so that Vivian knows that she is dealing with about fifteen inches of fucking thick prick! She remembers her husband and immediately relaxes. She can handle this cock.

Her pussy practically salivates now as the finger count inside it increases. By the time he gets to four, she has lost her mind. Vivian stretches her arms out in front of her on the desk as for the first time she is left with the feeling that she has no fucking control of what is happening to her. Bradley had always bordered this territory, and with every other man including her husband, she was in total control despite the roles that had been assumed. Tom was unequivocally the master of this ceremony.

It took Tom almost five minutes to find the inside of Vivian's vagina with his entire tool. It took some coaching, a hell of a lot of tongue and finger pussy-persuading, but eventually, the stubborn snatch gave way. And when it did, there was no stopping Tom from fucking the black off of Vivian. He fucked her so hard that there was no ducking the three massive orgasms she had before he finally shot a full load straight up inside her. They were both too fucking horny to care that there would be some admin for Vivian after. She herself didn't care too much about the admin though; a quick pill would make it like it never happened.

———

Selene walks in to find Vivian with an almost guilty smile on her face. She looks like someone on a diet who's been caught with a piece of chocolate in her mouth. They discuss the business at hand and Selene is given some of the tips that had been given to Christina. The same aggressive handling would be required, but Selene would obviously not go as far as Christina might, should the circumstance present itself. The meeting ends with Vivian feeling a little less guilty, the possibilities of the commissions from this business the best of anyone in the office at the moment.

CHAPTER 1

CHRISTINA IS a vision of young Hollywood when she walks into John Lionel's house for a briefing. Immediately John knows that Vivian has had more than just a hand in this transformation. He leads an obviously more aggressive Christine into his study. John has a hard time keeping his eyes on the pictures in the folder presented to him. His entire focus is the transformed Christine who smells exactly like Vivian and so has his cock rock hard.

She has a salmon suit on, Prada. It's a conservative length, but the tease of her hose disappearing under the pink just above her knee is almost too much for John. He leans over her and hopes that his own cologne has as dramatic an effect on her that hers has had on him because the thought of letting her leave his study now without first eating her cunt out is an almost impossibility now. He manages briefly to respond sensibly to the questions filtering up to him from Christina, who sits in his high-back leather chair.

"You've done something different with your hair," He can only whisper.

"I've done something different with everything." Her ego needed him to notice.

"It's nice." John wants to be touching her now, badly.

"Thank you, sir." Christina is aware of his desire for her and plays on their age difference by adding *sir* to the ends of her sentences now, turning John on even more. Unknown to John, this is her intention, her fondness for older men dancing in her groin while the contents of her folder occupy her head.

Fortunately, the air conditioning in the room cools the sweat on her neck and brow before it forms fully. It's not as gracious with John, who sweats uncontrollably until he has to unbutton half his shirt, revealing a rather hairy chest.

"I'm sorry; the air conditioning isn't helping me much against this heat." He makes an excuse as he realizes how wet his shirt is.

"We can take a break for a minute if you need to cool down sir, you're my only appointment this morning." Christina's offer is perfectly timed.

A pitcher of ice tea is brought in for them, offering welcome relief. John sits on his desk and runs a finger across the length of his cock, which has run out of room in his pants. He pretends to be making simple adjustments to his large meat, but he is hoping that the size and firmness of his dick will convince the young woman whose eyes have followed his fingers that he will be more than worth the effort. John is at that age where he needs such validations.

"What guarantees do I have that what I'm about to do won't have an adverse effect on the reason I'm really here?" Christina has really transformed into a mini version of her boss.

"And what is it that you might be thinking of doing

young miss?" John hopes that he knows, already unbuttoning the rest of his shirt.

Christina stands up from the chair and places a hand on each of John's knees. She bends over and opens her mouth over the bulge in his pants and takes a gentle bite. A few more bites and John needs to get his dick out. Christina helps him with this task, something that requires him to get off the table and stand so that his pants can be brought down to his knees. His dick is solid and impressive and obviously a show-off. She immediately takes it into her mouth.

Watching her work his cock just sends the rod into a frenzy and John starts fucking her mouth hard. Christina maintains her composure, understanding his excitement. She lets him hold her head and work her mouth around on his dick for a long while before she pulls on his balls and releases his meat from her mouth. She knows from her experience with older men that the best fucks are the ones where they're in control. She stands in front of him with a *'now what'* look in her doe eyes.

John runs an affectionate finger over her lips. She can't help taking the finger into her mouth, whereupon John feeds her two more. He enjoys how accommodating her mouth is. His other hand feels up her thigh under her skirt. Her hose forms a thin barrier between his fingers and her cunt, but what he can ascertain over the sheer fabric shielding her pussy is that she has a fat and probably very juicy vagina. *He really wants it now!*

John understands the delicate nature of women's clothing and gets down on his knees. He removes Christina's shoes and then carefully slides her hose down, placing them on the chair behind her. Her skirt is unzipped and removed next before John stands up and gets her out of her blouse, the blazer having been carried in and never worn. In her bra and panties, there is no way back now. John fumbles with his own shoes and a minute later are completely naked and removing Christina's bra. Her g-string is left for last and is removed skilfully with his teeth, bringing him right back down to his knees.

He takes a very long sniff of her snatch. Christina grabs feebly onto his hair which gives way between her fingers. So instead she takes firm hold of his head. As soon as she does he tilts his head back slightly, parts her legs, and settles his mouth on her vagina, giving the swelling, moistening cunt the most delicious French kiss. Christina's pussy opens itself up immediately to the assault.

After sucking on her cunt for the longest time John starts to taste the first trickles of her juices. He takes hold of his cock and gives it a steady beating as the scent and taste of Christina fill not only his mouth and nose but also the entire room. The more he strokes his dick the more his cock wants the inside of Christina. She keeps throwing her eyes to the folder, hoping that this isn't a mistake. But deep down inside her, she knows despite her naivety that this is exactly what Vivian was grooming her for. This is the promise that was made in her absence that led to StarStruck's retention of John Lionel's business. Christina resolves immediately to enjoy the shit out of being Vivian's whore.

She takes John's finger into her easily despite the tightness of her cunt. This has more to do with the force with which he inserts it though. He fingers her cunt with the expertise of every cock that has ever fucked her, and better in fact than most she can remember. He moves in and out of her hard and she plants her feet on the wooden floor to keep herself standing. John fingers her ass simultaneously and in twenty fantastic minutes, she has a massive orgasm, pleasing John immensely. He takes his tongue to task on her thighs and all the way back up to her pussy, cleaning up the consequences of his finger invasion.

The view over the grounds from the study window is in a word, amazing. Leaning on the ledge, with her back and ass to the room, Christina soaks in the sight. She also enjoys the breeze blowing through the lattice that is for the most part see-through. John's tongue runs firmly down the inside of her butt cheeks several times before a wet finger slides into the hole. He stands straight now as he fingers her butthole, holding her steady at the hip with his other hand. He considers for a moment adding another finger but she just responds so favorably to the one appendage drilling into her anus that he decides not to upset what is a very erotic vision.

After positioning himself behind her he slides his dick into he pussy which is already drizzling *lady lube* on the wood. He manages to get his entire cock into her at a slight angle without compromising the work he is doing in her ass. This double fuck is enough for Christina to yell out his name in complete and total ecstasy for the full four hours he fucks her in this position. She has thirteen orgasms by the time the fantastically competent John Lionel has his first and only one. He follows this up by washing her hair, along with the rest of her in his shower, ordering a fresh suit for her, feeding her sushi, and signing off on enough real estate business to earn Christina $200 000 in agent commissions over the next couple of months.

The vivid descriptions Christina gives to Vivian the next morning are enough to wet Vivian's snatch considerably. She pretends to be impressed with the agent's performance but doesn't need to pretend at all about being pleased with the business. That John wasted no time fucking the transformed Christina offends Vivian somewhat. She suddenly wants him, not because he's had Christina, but because she needs to confirm for him that *she* is better. This thought consumes her and the rest of her meeting with Christina is lost. She requests a written report about the business part of the meeting and dismisses the young woman who has managed, with no help this time, to look even more like a younger, whiter, Vivian Washington.

In his gym, John has a hard-on just thinking of the twenty-two-year-old pussy that milked his python. Every part of him wants more of it, and as long as he has players buying property, he'll have his share. The part of him that desires Vivian, the arrogant egotistical part, hasn't vanished though. But he will continue to fuck Christina for a while he resolves, knowing that her youth will have her confessing to her *mother superior* every time. Hopefully, this will be the motivation required to get Vivian Washington's legs parted and his milky bar moving deep inside her dark chocolate.

CHAPTER 2

HER OBSESSION with proving herself to John consumes her after the third week of juicy feedback from Christina. So before Bradley arrives for their regular appointment Vivian has left StarStruck and made her way, unannounced, to John's house. Upon arrival, she finds Christina's car in the drive. She lets herself in without using the doorbell and makes a point of avoiding the staff. Vivian goes in the direction of where she knows the master bedroom to be.

The door is wide open, the bed not visible from the hall. She enters the room quietly, walking on her hose for the sounds made by her heels on the wood. The sight of John fucking a bound Christina on his Victorian four-poster turns her on. He is a very hairy man, but the rips of his toned body are difficult to hide despite this. Christina's body is perfect, and Vivian immediately hates her. Watching John move deep in and then out of her, and her moving around underneath him, receiving him and not resisting despite her restraints, the total loss of her youth suddenly hits Vivian and she can't bring herself to watch. She uses the same stealth to leave the house, *unnoticed*.

Unfortunately for Vivian, even if no human caught her moving in and out of the house, John's security system did. The cameras are so well hidden that even John often forgets where they are. But when his groundsman admires the silver Porsche that was in the drive yesterday, John has to check the tapes to confirm what he already knows. And as expected, Vivian Washington was in his house yesterday. She was in his hallway, and in his bedroom. So he knows that she saw him with Christina. The next move now has to be hers. He doesn't want to do or say anything that might insult the woman his ego still wants him to fuck.

Despite even his best efforts now, Bradley is unable to fully satisfy Vivian. After a little more than a month of fucking him he has shown himself to be a bit of a one-trick pony. And Bradley's trick is the size of his dick, something Vivian can access on tap at home, her husband having a super-sized cock himself. Her focus is on John Lionel now, and even Bradley can feel that her attention is elsewhere. She simply goes through the motions with him, not entirely unpleasant, but he doesn't like the absence of her '*wanting him*'.

"Is there a problem Vivian?" He braves finally.

"No Bradley, no problem. Things are just a little overwhelming for me at work and at home so I'm sorry if I seem a little absent. But don't worry, you're the one thing that I look forward to each morning." She tries to give him the straightest face possible and Bradley decides to accept what she says. He knows that there is at least no chance that she is fucking someone else in the office, and that her husband is fucking her each night is something he has made peace with already. This arrangement has nothing to do with emotions after all.

At home, Randy notices that his wife is a little more separated from him than usual. They've never actually discussed the rift that has developed between them over the years, both of them secretly hoping that it will just get better. Randy was busy setting up and running his business, and Vivian was busy growing hers. There has just never been a need to get emotionally involved in a situation that was managed by regular, but boring sex. So regardless of their disconnect, they seem to have an arrangement to fuck even on the days that they say barely five words to each other.

Of course, Vivian doesn't need this booty call from the hubby. She is fucked every morning by reliable *Brad*, and every afternoon by whoever she wants. There is no way of course that Randy doesn't know that his wife is getting it elsewhere unless he doesn't care for her at all. But he absolutely loves her, which is why he stays with her and, despite the obvious signs fed to him from his cock, each night he dutifully fucks Vivian. Yes, he gets to fuck her each night, but the only courtesy and honor he has been that he is simply the last man to fuck her each day.

Randy keeps himself busy online. He knows that he has an impressive cock, so he locks himself in his den pretending to be playing poker with virtual gamblers. What he is actually doing is beating his meat to his webcam in full view of a bevy of very appreciative college girls, housewives, and homosexuals who all touch themselves from arousal to orgasm at the sight of the massive meaty ebony rod. This attention affirms his manhood and he is able to go upstairs and send a firm cock into his wife nightly and without fail, so neither of them has a reason to make an audible complaint.

They've said no more than the usual *hello* and *how was your day* to each other tonight, but Randy finds a showered Vivian naked and on her back in their bed by the time he's cleaned his cock and walked up the four flights to their bedroom. He hated finding her already undressed because one of the things about having a wife with a banging body that turned him on more than even the actual body was the process of revealing it. He loved unwrapping her, the way he had done on their wedding night. But something had happened on *that night*, the *happiest night of their lives*, their *wedding night* that led to the systematic breakdown of their sex life. Randy has no idea still what this is, and Vivian is giving no insights.

He is quick about removing his own clothing, taking just the time from the door to the bed to be totally naked. His cock hangs low between his legs, full length but flaccid. He gets on the bed and is on top of Vivian in two movements, his length allowing this. Randy kisses her neck first, the smell of her having the same effect on him as it did on John. Then his lips are on her face, kissing her cheeks gently and then her lips. The feeling of his mouth on hers moistens her cunt deep inside and removes all memories of whoever happened to fuck her today. This day it had just been the usual fifteen minutes of Bradley.

Randy's love is always overridden briefly by his ego and manhood. He takes a dry finger and sends it slowly into his wife. Vivian's pussy always tightens more or less over his finger depending on how many times she'd been fucked on any particular day. This is something he figured out on their honeymoon, where despite the sudden 'change' in Vivian, there was an average of seven or eight fuck sessions a day.

Randy would tease her by sending a finger into her to check the *temperature*, and after a few days, he learned the inner workings of his wife's cunt. He hadn't thought then that that test would now be used to check who else had been inside her, and how many times.

He ignores the results and slowly fingers Vivian until her vagina becomes moist and then wet. He never stops kissing her while he uses just one finger to prepare her pussy for his now solid cock. It takes ten minutes of fingering for her to drool from her pussy onto the sheets. She's ready for penetration. He takes a minute though to lick up the generous flow, knowing that as long as he doesn't dry out the inside of her pussy she'll be fine. Of course, he knows in the man part of himself that she's probably given cock similar to his a run, and he only wishes that his cock could once more be given the same treatment. But more than just his cock, he wants to be loved by her, even if only half as much as he loves her.

Randy's cock eases into her slowly, and Vivian adjusts underneath him. She's had his length before, in a couple of other men. But the thickness, the girth of Randy's rod is at least an inch more than any dick she has ever had. It takes a further twenty minutes for her to be settled enough for him to fuck her in swift strokes until first she, and then he cums in a heated heap on the grey satin sheets. They clean up in their own part of the 'his and hers' bathroom and then fall asleep after exchanging light loveless pecks on each other's cheeks.

The sun catches her face tenderly as Vivian peeps out of her corner office window. She thinks briefly of her fuck last night, and of the blowjob, she gave Randy this morning. He

reciprocated with a rapid licking of her pussy, a swift swallowing of its contents, and then his usual coffee and bagel.
Bradley has also just left her with a feeling between her legs
no more magical than what Randy had done. All she has on
her mind is the look on John Lionel's face after he has
fucked her and realized that she is indeed the undeniable
fuck of the millennium. She needs this to happen fast. She
needs this to happen *today!*

She sets up a meeting with John through his assistant
and then makes a spa appointment. Taking into account
everything that she had done for Christina she uses this as a
base. A few added treatments turns her into a fresh flame of
melting chocolate wrapped in hints and whispers of vanilla
and berries. The light summer frock, cut to just above her
knee, hangs over her curves and then gives way to her legs.
The fabric is light enough for her to feel like she's wearing
nothing but heavy enough to just about hint at the fact that
she is wearing absolutely nothing underneath it. For the first
time in more than four months, she also has her hair loose
outside of her husband's bed.

John is in the middle of a lap across his swimming pool
when Vivian is shown to the pool deck. The spread on the
table is the only indication that she is expected, and so
Vivian accepts a goblet of pomegranate juice from which
she manages a single sip before John makes a perfect exit
from the black pool just as the golden sunset wraps around
every part of him. The water runs off him in a rhythm that
loses Vivian briefly in an imaginary symphony. By the time
she's gathered herself she's taking a second sip and John is
drying himself right in front of her. He has nothing but a
Speedo on, and even after they've greeted and sat down he
chooses not to put on the robe hanging on his chair.

They both know why Vivian is here, it hangs thick in

the air. In his tight, wet Speedos John's cock is already hard.
Vivian too is wet under the nothing of her dress, but she is
calm and proceeds professionally with the faux update of
John and his team's property acquisitions. They speak for
just under an hour before the evening breeze and the darkness moves them inside. Vivian has another pomegranate
ice tea while John excuses himself and goes to his bedroom
to get changed. It takes her the entire drink before she
decides that she has nothing to lose by following him
upstairs.

John is naked on his bed, pulling on his cock when
Vivian walks in. He knew she would come. She walks in,
her eyes fixed on his thick meat. The hair on his body takes
her back somewhat. Black women are not accustomed to so
much fur. She stands by his bed, none of them saying a
word. John hopes that he is able to satisfy her, and so does
she. Vivian needs only for him to deem her better than any
he's ever had. This is all she's come here for, to lay claim to a
title she's decided she deserves. This is about to be a
meeting of two of Texas's most arrogant.

He sits up and takes hold of her thighs. Lifting her dress
he is greeted by perfectly shaven pussy. There is no sign on
Vivian that a thread of hair has ever grown there. Her clit is
thick and full. It looks delicious and John tastes it. He licks
it repeatedly while she lifts the dress over her head and
drops it carefully on the floor. John is already doing one of
her favorite things while she herself still has no clue how
she is going to please him. John is drunk from the flavor of
her fanny and he pulls her onto the bed, lays her on her
back, parts her legs, and goes deeper into her with his
tongue for a more satisfying drink.

Vivian cannot concentrate on anything but the
powerful tongue in her pussy. John knows that he has found

her weakness and this power hardens his cock. She pulls on John and his sheets in turn as he keeps pulling more and more from her cunt with the suction that is his mouth. Nothing can stop her from spraying her load now and she wonders too late if maybe she should warn him. But it's too late, and out of Vivian's vagina shoots a fountain of fluid that fills John's mouth so fast he pulls away to check what is going on.

As soon as he realizes that she is having an orgasm, he is immediately impressed with himself, taking full credit for her excessive climax. He sends a finger into her past the liquid shooting out of her hole and he plugs it up. He fingers her pussy, fiery hot much to his delight, before pulling out the finger so as to watch the fountain again. He plugs up the fountain several times until her pussy simply trickles a steady stream from where once it gushed. They exchange a look that says to both of them that the games have now begun. John gives Vivian's cunt a good sucking and then licks it clean before laying on his back and holding his cock up, pointing it towards her. It's her turn.

But instead of taking the beautiful penis into her mouth, Vivian stands on the bed astride John and pulls on her own clit. She milks herself using her fingertips while John pulls on his balls. He is so turned on by the sight that he is scared that if he touches his cock he might shoot prematurely. John has incredible stamina. But he can only manage one ejaculation a day. Vivian sends two of her own fingers into her pussy and then comes all the way down into a squat so that her ass brushes over John's balls and cock. She runs herself over him, to and fro, increasing his desire to be inside her, the fact that the entrance to her pussy is blocked driving him insane. She adds another finger as she stands up again and fingers herself almost violently for ten minutes until her pussy rains over John's chest, wetting him almost as much as his pool had.

Vivian brings her pussy down over John's mouth at his pleading and he eats out the excess. She leans towards his cock and slides her mouth over it completely. What she does to his dick is so unexpected that John shudders and shivers underneath Vivian. She seems to suck and lick his dick all at once. Her tongue dances across the entire surface of his shaft and also tickles and tantalizes his head. John shakes uncontrollably now, totally unexpected to him, and he tries to brace himself by pulling Vivian tightly onto his face and sucking on her cunt harder. So overwhelming is her mouth on his meat that it is only Vivian who knows that John has just shot a massive load into her mouth. She knows this because she has to take a deep breath before swallowing his heated flow.

It takes a minute for her to lift her cunt free of John, but Vivian manages to get herself between his legs so she can lick his balls. She takes them into her mouth, sucking on them and then licking and biting, nibbling his nuts gently. John gives his cock a look and realizes as the last trickles of his cum run down the still solid shaft that he has had an orgasm. He takes hold of his dick and looks at Vivian with a question in his eye. He decides that what she doesn't know won't hurt her, and instead of letting her know that he's probably shot the only load he's gonna shoot today, he takes full advantage of his firm cock. He pulls her up to him and splits her legs over his cock.

The urgency surprises Vivian but she hides it. She allows John to feed his cock into her vagina and move her around on it. He seems to move in millimeters under her as he rotates her on his cock. It takes a full hour of stirring her on his dick this way for him to edge towards climax. They both have a massive and largely unexpected orgasm that again sees John shudder and shake under a thoroughly satisfied Vivian. John rests his head on his hands and observes Vivian on top of him. He can't help but tell her that she is the first woman in ten years to pull a double whammy from him. This is all she needs to hear.

Without asking for his permission, Vivian starts to move slowly over John's cock, now at half-mast. She dances her pussy gently on his dick and pulls on her breasts as they heave high and low in full view of John. He takes deep breaths, not sure if what she is obviously attempting is possible. But since his cock is cooperating for the most part, and since there is no sign of pain or discomfort, he relaxes into her effort. In less than ten minutes Vivian has soaked his groin in her juice, his own juice joining her flow a minute later. He has a look of complete disbelief on his face. She is happy with the outcome.

Christina notices the same disconnect with John over the following weeks that Bradley and even Randy are feeling with Vivian. Everyone at StarStruck is acutely aware also of a happier Vivian. She hasn't slept with John again though, declining his many invitations. His gifts start to fill her office until Bradley becomes aware of an admirer. Christina is the first though to make the association between the lavish gifts being delivered to Vivian's office, and John Lionel. The realization that John, *her John*, is now wanting to and probably already is fucking aging Vivian is almost too much for her to handle. In the naivety of youth, Christina resolves to get Vivian back, *and seduce Randy!*

CHAPTER 3

THE OPPORTUNITY for her seduction presents itself sooner than she had thought it would. Christina had been discussing renovations to a property that she had just convinced one of John's newest recruits to buy. All Star-Struck's renovations and construction requirements were contracted to Hall Construction, Randy's company. After a meeting with the client at his offices, Christina stays behind to get clarity on some budgetary details. Randy has no idea what *details* she *actually* has in mind.

Christina has maintained her mini-me version of Vivian's appearance, something that Randy notices more subliminally than anything. The most striking similarity though is her perfume. Every time Christina moves, the fans in the room carry her scent deep into Randy's nose, and down into the parts of him that long for his wife. His cock responds to the woman in his head and heart more than to the woman now bending over him, pointing to the options for the balustrades on a staircase they're considering. There is no way to hide the massive erection in his pants before Christina sees it.

"Wow," she says seductively.

"I'm sorry," Randy is apologetic for what he thinks is offending her.

"Don't be." Christina runs her fingers along the full length of his cock. "Wow," she repeats.

Randy closes his eyes and imagines that the hands on his dick are his wife's. This is easy given the generous doses of Vivian's perfume feeding into him from Christina. There is no turning back once she has exposed his dick, once her mouth has found her way on to it, once she is moving up and down on the serpent and bringing it so close to shooting that Randy pulls her off his dick so as not to drench her in cum. Christina lifts her skirt, pulls her panties to the side, and kisses Randy on his lips while he eases his cock into her pussy. He lets her work the shaft into her pussy herself because it is obvious despite her aggression that his dick is more than she's ever had to manage.

It takes Christina an hour to finally get moist enough for two-thirds of Randy to be inside her. By this time Randy is lost in the tightness, the freshness of this cunt, his first pussy that isn't his wife's since he met her. It's not so much that he is enjoying it now, not as much as he enjoys Vivian even now that they're fucking is dutiful at best. Randy is simply determined not to embarrass Christina after all the effort she's put in already. He starts to thrust into her, careful not to feed her more than she can handle. Christina is almost immediately thrown into orgasm by the thrusting of this massive black tool in her perfectly fragile pink pussy.

Randy takes the reigns now completely from Christina and stands up without removing his cock from her. He places her on his desk and tells her to hold on to him. She does, and he thrusts his dick into her until several more inches make it into her cunt. Christina can't help but look down at the action in her vagina. It's a beautiful sight. Randy closes his eyes and focuses intently on completing Christina's climax. He does this expertly and then pulls his cock from her. She draws his orgasm from him with her mouth and swallows his warm, generous load. Randy is a gentleman, having a coffee and a chat with Christina once they've cleaned up. There seems to be no reason to voice their intention to keep this from Vivian. Christina is less than content with her vengeance.

A side-effect of being a first-time cheater is that the guilt has a profound effect on your ability to attend. Over the next couple of weeks, Randy is more than attentive to every need his wife has. He sends her gifts to the office and greets her with gifts at home. He makes love to her not once, but twice and sometimes three or four times a night. Even his love-making is more intense, more focused on her pleasure, and often he doesn't cum until the last round. His behavior convinces Vivian of the very thing Randy is trying to conceal. She knows that he's fucked someone else. Of course, there is absolutely nothing that she can say to him, her own sins a heavy presence in her mind.

What this does for her is unexpected. Vivian realizes that she is actually still very much in love with her husband. In fact, Vivian finds that each day she falls more and more in love with Randy in different ways. Not that this in any way inconveniences Bradley, she keeps that appointment. But there is suddenly less and less of an allure for her to pounce on any other cock. The only cock that still lingers in her head is John's. But since she's done with him what her ego needed, there is little excitement left there with the old, hairy Mr. Lionel. This frustrates John to the end that he finds it increasingly difficult to be satisfied by Christina.

The happier Vivian seems the more pissed off Christina gets. It doesn't help her much that Randy is suddenly all business, and she has seen more of her own finger in her pussy than she has of John's dick over the last while. But Vivian seems to be getting the best of every world, Randy and his mammoth dick, John, and even, if the sounds from her office this morning are anything to go by, Bradley too. Her youth seems to be no match for Vivian's experience, and Christina is forced to admit that no matter what she thinks of her, Vivian Washington is a fucking stunning woman.

Christina cannot know of course that John has not had a second go at Vivian. He too is as frustrated about Vivian as she is about Randy. Not that Christina wants Randy. She just wants what Vivian has since she has fucked up what had looked like something good with John. Even now as John fingers her in the coolness of his swimming pool Christina can't help but feel that he wishes she was someone else. So she too wills herself to imagine that John is in fact, Randy. It is very difficult to do, especially with her eyes open. So she closes them while encouraging John to add a few more fingers to her pussy.

Three fingers in her cunt are still not enough. She smiles at John and urges him on, encouraging a forth. He looks at her, concerned. She smiles, stroking his dick under the water while she forces his fingers deeper into herself. John eventually obliges, and four thick fingers fuck Christina until she screams in ecstasy. John needs to own this screaming so he pulls his fingers from her and forces his cock into her hard. There is no time for her to question this change in the game plan as John fucks her hard and savagely, wanting to give her the pleasure his fingers obviously were. Christina loves this power fucking and has multiple orgasms at the hands of a frustrated John.

She doesn't spend the night. There is a new determination she has to have Randy, just once more. The reason for this is that John, several times, *called her Vivian*. Everything that Ms. Washington has ever done for her is suddenly a vague memory and all she wants now is to hurt her. Actually what she wants is to be her. She wants to be a woman that can turn the whole world upside down with the sway of her hips and the curve of her breasts. She wants to be able to speak a single word through perfect lips and have millions handed her on a platter. She wants the power. But this isn't possible. Christina knows this. So she decides that she will at the very least take some of Vivian's shine away.

Randy is still largely unresponsive to Christina's advances. They have more and more meetings though as the renovations become a reality and more and more details need to be finalized. Christina is the last person that Vivian would expect her husband to cheat on her with. She knows from their early days at college that Randy was a sister's man. He had often, as had his friends, said that he had no attraction to white females. Of course, people change, and Randy did have his own set of curiosities. But he had never acted on them before, unlike his wife. Christina was desperate for one more go with the python, something that Randy was not keen on apparently.

Today Christina has discarded her make-over completely. She wears a comfortable summer dress, a wrap that ties on the side. It covers her almost completely but is of such a light fabric that she feels naked. She has crisp under-wear on that makes her comfortable and feel sexy all at once. She enters the Hall Construction office and waits for Randy to offer her a seat. He offers her a drink too, obviously thrown by her lack of makeup or effort. For the first time since he met her Christina looks young and fresh, almost innocent and virginal. Whether her intention or not, Randy suddenly wants to make love to her.

Christina plays the demure innocence card until it becomes obvious to her that she has found that part of Randy, that part that exists in any man actually, that has them need a vulnerable woman to take care of. He feels his cock, gives it a few squeezes and finds that it is thick but flaccid. He is not hardening. His head tells him that he wants to make the most beautiful love to the available woman in front of him, but his cock is not coming to the party. He knows that there is no need for a full erection to be able to penetrate a pussy. He knows that Christina's pussy is tender and penetrable. But he also knows somehow that the lack of an erection will insult her.

He gets on his knees in front of her and decides to initiate, to confirm to the young woman suddenly appearing insecure that she is indeed desirable. He lets his hand stray under her long covering and she parts her legs as his fingers reach her pussy. He enters her with a thick gentle finger and bites into her thighs as he fingers her deep and hard. Slowly his dick starts to harden, and before long he has a full erection that he frees from his pants. He has all the equipment now to give Christina an afternoon she won't forget.

Pulling on the string at the side of Christina's dress he releases it. She stands naked in front of him and for the first time and Randy allows himself to truly appreciate her body.

Christina is suddenly not a sin he commits against his wife, but a gift he is giving himself for all of Vivian's. In all the years that he had known of his wife's infidelity, he had never thought to get even. And even now, had it not been for Christina's candid revelations of Vivian's rendezvous with John and Bradley, Randy would firstly not have agreed to this meeting, and he would definitely not have by-passed his faithful husband programming and replaced it with his '*I have a fucking huge dick and this tender young thing deserves a real taste of it as much as I deserve a real go at her punani*' program.

Randy makes love to Christina for seven hours before he finally makes his way home to his wife. He goes straight to the shower and then straight to bed. Vivian doesn't wake him, although, with his recent loving and attention, it does bother her that he has not even waited to say good night. She has been feeling closer to him over the last while and it had seemed like they were making progress towards each other. But tonight she gets nothing.

She can't help checking his clothes but there is absolutely no sign that he was with another woman. So she gets back into bed and reminds herself that she had thoroughly enjoyed her nine o clock with Bradley. She smiles at the memory of the gift John had sent her today despite her having told him it would never happen again. Vivian looks at her husband, large and handsome. She loves him, deeply. But there is something inside her that needs the distance. Randy hasn't given up on them it seems, he's still here. It seems unfair what she's been doing and she feels tinges of guilt, but she isn't ready to face about it. The power-player in her feels no need to explain herself anyway, not even to herself. Randy on the other hand sleeps with just one thought in his head. He believes Christina, if he didn't he wouldn't have made such passionate love to her. But he does need one thing for him to know how he is going to navigate the rest of his marriage. He needs to get conclusive proof that Vivian is fucking around. He needs to catch her in the act.

CHAPTER 4

CHRISTINA IS MORE than eager to help Randy. Her twenty-two-year-old head tells her that if Randy sees his wife getting fucked by John, she will both win him over and completely fuck with Vivian, or Randy will beat the shit out of John and he will have no choice but to run to her for the requisite wound licking and ego-stroking. This is not completely unlikely but to approach the completely unreliable scenario with the certainty of either outcome is at best juvenile.

John sends Vivian another gift that peaks her interest but just; A Chanel suit and an invitation to dinner that promises to be worth her while. There can be nothing more attractive to a woman than a Chanel suit, and the dinner has sparked her curiosity. Vivian packs all the gifts into a bag except for the suit, which she wears. She drives to John's house wondering what it could be that he assumes that will have her intrigued.

The soft grey of the Chanel would have been almost corporate if it didn't fit Vivian so well. Also, the light silver accessories she's chosen turn the skirt and ruffled blouse into an elegant cocktail ensemble. John wears a pair of chinos and Prada sandals with a light white Gucci shirt. He looks like he's expected her to turn up just as she has because they match each other almost perfectly. The problem is that John is not expecting Vivian. He's expecting Christina. Christina's is the handwriting on the note Vivian received.

John's surprise comes across as forced, so Vivian thinks he's having her on. He insists he hasn't sent her the suit or the invitation and says that he would never have put that color on her anyway. She laughs while accepting a drink from him, a virgin daiquiri, and asks after the news that he said would be worth her while. Still, John tells her that he made no such promise. He is about to get deeper into explaining himself without mentioning Christina when his phone rings. Christina apologizes profusely and is unable to make the dinner that she herself had arranged with him.

Opportunity is not something that John lets slip by on any day, and Vivian in Chanel is an opportunity he is not going to let slip by. A sly smile finds its way onto his face and Vivian is suddenly comfortable, assuming that she is right and that he has just been playing with her. He has a thick drink while he tries to think of something that could satisfactorily qualify as a profound piece of information that would warrant him having her drive all this way. Nothing comes to him.

"I really want to touch you, Vivian..."

"I know. Is this why I'm here?"

"No. Not entirely."

"John we've been through this every day, for the last while. What happened was a mistake. It should never have..."

"I respect that. But you need to understand just how easy it is for a man to develop a love affair with your vagina."

"Just my vagina?"

"That's the only part of you that's available 'Mrs. Washington"

The hint at emotion confuses Vivian. It softens her to the possibility of giving John one more dive into her snatch. He wasn't a bad fuck. And he has been persistent. In Vivian's world, persistence always paid off. So, for the last time, before she hands John over completely to Christina, StarStruck having already banked some serious cash from his business, she decides to indulge the hairy beast. Anything that comes now from Christina's pussy's association with John Lionel's cock will be a bonus.

They decide at Vivian's suggestion then to skip dinner, since time would not be on their side if they went through each of the elaborate courses prepared in John's kitchen. He takes her into his study, a bonus for Christina and Randy who sit in John's basement security room watching the live play. She had hoped at best that they would catch the pair walking into John's bedroom, the rest left to the imagination but obvious. However, in the study, there are strategically placed cameras to protect the sensitive contents of the room's three safes. Randy is suddenly nervous, not wanting the visual confirmation of what he's known for years.

For the next two hours, Randy watches his wife being undressed. He watches another man's cock move in and out of her mouth. He watches another's tongue over her cunt, licking her clit, digging into her vagina. Randy watches Vivian fucked every which way and then some. His only relief is that there is no sound feed; Christina disabled it, just to stop herself from having to listen to her John saying *her* name. By the time Randy is back from that place in his head where he pulls each of John's fingernails out slowly before using a blow torch on his nuts, he asks to leave. Christina copies the tape to her mobile while Randy revels in his misery with his head low between his legs and then they make an inconspicuous exit.

Vivian arrives home to find the house in darkness. Somewhere under the hum of the fridge is the clicking on a keypad. She knows that the sound comes from her husband's lair. She walks down the dark staircase to the basement and pushes the door open slightly. Inside her husband is naked, leaning back on his chair, the light on his webcam on. He strokes his cock slowly, sensuously, obviously a performance. On the screen several windows are open, the windows filled with thighs and cunts, fingers and dildos moving in and out of the many pussies her husband is beating his meat to. This is so unlike Randy that Vivian can't help but enter the room.

"And this?" She asks.

"Go to bed Vivian, good night," He says coldly.

Every part of her tells her that going to bed would be the best thing for her.

Three packages are on her desk when Vivian arrives at the office the next morning. She ignores them for a long while, wondering why Randy wasn't in bed when she woke up. She tried twice to get him on his phone but there was no answer. Vivian assumes that she's forgotten an appointment he told her about over the last while and so her focus falls on the packages. She opens them with the distracted irritation she's had each time she's opened one of John's gifts. But these are not from John.

The first item, the lightest, is a letter. Christina has resigned with immediate effect. The second package is a disc. On it is a two-hour recording of John Lionel fucking the absolute *bajeezus* out of her. The attached note informs her that her husband has seen this tape. The third disc is also a recording, of Randy making the most delicious love to none other than Christina. Vivian places the items in an order that makes better sense to her. She watches a few minutes of her and Lionel, then Randy and Christina, and then reads the letter that sights '*stunted growth prospects*' as the reason for her leaving. Vivian cancels her appointment with Bradley, indefinitely.

It's 9 PM before Vivian finally decides that she will not be calling Christina and that she will be making her way home to deal with her husband. She has no idea what to expect. What she knows is that the way Randy touched Christina hurts her. She hates being hurt. But she also knows that he probably felt the same way when he watched her being fucked by John. She doesn't think too hard about it and before leaving the office she destroys the discs, not too concerned that there might be copies. She drops off the letter on the desk of her HR head and heads home.

Inside their living room, Randy has a calm expression on his face. The drink in his hand is uncharacteristic for the ex-jock, but he needs it to avoid jumping straight into an argument. He has never faced or fought with Vivian before and so he has no idea what a fight between them would constitute. Randy takes another sip as Vivian enters, puts down her bag, and sits directly opposite him. They are separated by a sea of mohair on the marble floor.

"So you know," Vivian's controlling personality requires her to start.

"I'm not stupid Vivian I've always known," Randy won't tolerate being patronized.

"And now," Vivian asks.

"Now I don't know Vivian. I just don't know. I'd know if I didn't love you. But I love you!"

"I love you too Randy," She's honest.

"Then why?"

"I don't know"

"Don't give me that Vivian, why?" Randy is not going to let this go now. It's been years coming.

The tension in the room suddenly lifts as honesty replaces all defenses. There is no more room for lies despite the double volumes of the space. Vivian's walls all come down in the presence of her husband and she reveals to him all the insecurities of her youth. She discloses her obsession with the *wedding* and her lack of preparation for the *marriage*. She tells Randy how in all honesty he was just the first man who asked her and so she married him. He was just her excuse for a wedding. But then she fell in love with him. It was just so hard for her to break out of the psychological place she had built for herself where she wanted everyone but Randy.

Randy gets up and leaves without saying a word. He is hurt. He hates that he was convenient for the most part of his married life. But what he doesn't doubt is that he has always and still does love Vivian. But she has confessed what he hadn't thought to be the reason for her sexual curiosities. He hates that now the last thing that is needed is for them to make love because sex means anything but love to Vivian. Randy spends most of the night walking the streets of their security estate trying to figure out how he can fix this.

"I think we need to bring someone into this." He finds Vivian in the same chair he left her. She's showered and in her pajamas though.

"Like a therapist?" The possibility that her marriage could be saved excites her.

"No, like another couple into our bed, to join us, for sex" Randy's speech is measured.

"What?" Vivian is confused.

"Let's not cheat on each other. Let's fuck other people in front of one another and see what it does to us. If we can honestly feel nothing, then we'll know what to do. If we feel something, anything, then we will take the necessary steps to fix this." Vivian can tell that this really has nothing to do with sex.

"Okay... who?" Vivian is prepared to try this, although exposing herself to another man in the presence of her husband already makes her uncomfortable.

"Selene and Tom. You know them." Randy is actually Tom's boss. And Tom had told him a while back about how he had fucked his wife's boss. Tom had since confessed to his wife, who had taken it better than he thought. She had said half-jokingly half-not that she was going to fuck Randy and then they could call it Even Stevens. This is the premise that the two men use to get Selene in on the plan when Randy calls them in for a *meeting* the next day.

Vivian and Selene have a chance to speak at the spa Randy books for them. They discuss the evening at length until the idea *settles*. This is going to just be a fun exploration between four adults. Massages and champagne have them relaxed and resembling friends by the time they leave and make their way to Vivian's house. They arrive and get into the most delicate negligee, nothing else. Hair brushed and running down their backs, they sit on the bed with a bottle of champagne, affirming their courage, turning it slowly into excitement.

Randy and Tom arrive to find their wives giggling on

the bed. They make quick work of the shower and don't bother getting dressed. Then both men give each other the once over, same height, almost exactly the same cock, the only difference is the color. They join their wives on the bed and start off with their own women, kissing, touching, fondling, and fingering. As soon as the heat is at its peak, the swop is made.

Vivian and Tom are known to each other. But even so, they are more awkward with one another than Selene and Randy. Tom spends an incredible amount of time sucking on Vivian's pussy. He eats her out with the patience of someone avoiding the escalation to the next step. The realization that he is busy with his boss's wife makes him visibly nervous. His nervousness though translates to expert oral and he brings Vivian to an orgasm in minutes. She can't get comfortable with Tom's cock in her mouth though and so Tom dives back into her pussy with his mouth.

Randy bites into Selene's thighs, and then her belly. He plants kisses on every part of her but her mouth. When his head settles between her legs he licks her clit. Selene shivers with each lap of his tongue on her. Randy digs his tongue into her cunt and feeds his saliva into her snatch at the same rate that her pussy produces its own juice. In just a few minutes she is wet and bordering a climax. Both Randy and Tom now have a single focus, the women underneath them.

Tom and Randy look at each other for permission before sending their cocks into each other's wives. While the presence in alternative pussy is exciting for their egos, the fucking is largely clinical. They put as much attention into it as possible, but despite the thorough enjoyment of it, the smell of their wives fusing with the smells of another man, right next to them, challenges them somewhat. Both men love their wives. The women feel the same but are at the mercy of the massive cocks pleasing every inch of their cunts. The pleasure briefly lifts them from the realization that it isn't their husbands fucking them.

After about an hour of fucking it becomes clear to both Randy and Tom that if they are to have any hope of awesome orgasms they will have to change strategy. After a few more deep thrusts each man reclaims his own wife. The comfort levels in the room are immediately elevated. Both couples lose themselves completely in each other and what follows is an hour of intense lovemaking. Multiple orgasms all round and Selene and Vivian are both left sucking on their husband's dicks for another hour, just to give their pussies a break.

They please their wives repeatedly, and their wives please their husbands in return. They manage over the course of the night to swop again, with greater success as they realize and confirm that the exploration is an extension of the love they have for one another. By the time Selene and Tom leave after breakfast the next day, there are arrangements made for another session. It is clear that this is a far better way for them to keep things interesting while they reignite their own fire. It will be a while before things get back to what they were before their wedding but at least now they are on the same journey towards the same end. Bradley finally accepts that he will not have Vivian on his own again, but appreciates Randy inviting him for a little male/male/female action, just to wean himself off of Vivian, whose fiery pussy is every bit as addictive as the hardest drug.

THE PROFESSOR

It isn't entirely impossible for her looks not to have played an integral part in landing Mariella Garrison the job as a junior professor of history at the University of Missouri. The skinny brunette has the figure of a European model, waif-like and ethereal. At thirty, she's almost too young for the Ph.D. she possesses, her lips full and red on her pastel face adding to her fresh youthful appearance. She looks no older than the 19-year-olds in her Introduction To World History class. She makes this the strength of her approach as she prepares herself for the 150 young minds that will be her responsibility this year. She's more concerned about her senior advisor though, a man of sixty with a taste for the vulnerable, new professors, *male or female*, he's mentored over the years.

Missouri is nothing like California, where Mariella grew up and went to school. As she stands naked in front of her mirror in her tiny apartment, a campus courtesy until she finds something more suitable, she wonders what to cover herself in so as not to make the wrong impression. But in the conservative state, the university having adopted this culture, it won't take much to make the wrong impression. Mariella isn't about to stress herself out about clothing though. She has two hours before her induction, and the campus administration building is a three-minute walk from her flat, so she sashays to the tiny kitchen, still in her *birthday suit*, and has another cup of coffee.

The chrome stool sends chills up her back through her ass. Her cheeks are hugged perfectly by the curve of the seat and so there isn't any urgency to separate herself from the chill. Instead, she takes another sip from her cup and counters the exterior shiver with some internal fire. From the kitchen window, Mariella takes in the view, park-like and perfect. She watches as birds and landscapers fight for first dibs on the night's produce left in the courtyard that separates learning from living. The sun is already up and she is glad now that she started in August. She imagines that the winters here will take some getting used to. Mariella watches as the sun traces from the floor, onto her foot, and then up her leg. She parts her legs and allows the sun to shine where it normally wouldn't.

The dark hair on her vagina soaks up the rays easily. Her cunt warms quickly and this warmth makes its way *inside her*. Wanting more heat she takes her cup and places it directly on her pussy. She closes her legs tight around the ivory cup and gives the remainder of the dark liquid inside it a stare. She dips her finger into it and is met with a much cooler sensation than she hopes. So the cup is back on the table and her legs are again parted in the direction of the sun so that her pussy can capitalize on the position of the kitchen window. In less than a minute, she is warming up again, her desire for fire growing fast.

Without too much thought she places her index finger on her clitoris. Touching herself is one of her favorite things to do. Mariella has never been one to throw herself under every man whose cock hardened at the sight of her. If she had, she'd have had more sex than *King Solomon*. So she chose to master the art of self-manipulation of her punani. Her finger on her clit sends the appropriate signals into her vagina and she circles her pink hard. She pushes onto it with her fingertip and applies ever-increasing pressure as her pussy starts to invite her inside itself.

Slowly her tip disappears into her cunt. The entry is easy, her cunt moist. She digs further into herself, her vagina almost pushing against her efforts because of her seated position. The pressure is intense, and Mariella pushes her finger further into herself. She craves another but if she's too ambitious she might end up in a horny heap on the kitchen floor. She was never the most coordinated, at least not outside of her bed. It makes no sense now to take unnecessary risks, despite her pleading pussy. So there's nothing to it, she's got enough time to take this to bed.

She's glad that she hasn't made it yet, and so she disappears under the covers. In the darkness, she sends her finger back into her pussy. Mariella pushes her cunt up into her fingers as she fucks herself hard. She adds two more fingers from one hand and rips into her pussy. Wet and wild, she adds three fingers from her other hand and pulls her pussy apart as if she is making room for a massive invader. There is no such invader in her bed so it's all up to her to get her pussy dealt with.

Mariella crosses her legs over her hands and squeezes her thighs together tightly. She fucks herself harder and harder with her fingers and lets her mind imagine a solid jock cock moving in and out of her. Her wild and very vivid imagination occasionally strays to older cock and it is her advisor fucking her. She manages at least to give him a fairly decent cock, strong and energetic, and it is this image of an undesirable man with a very desirable cock fucking her that actually gets her to orgasm. She takes deep breaths and then exhales loudly as she climaxes.

She uses her pink luminous dildo to bring herself to another orgasm in the shower. It's not just that she's suddenly super horny, a side effect of her anxiety, but she also doesn't want the last lingering thought to be of Senior Advisor Mark Stromberg fucking the shit out of her, and her enjoying it. So again she works hard to conjure up images of jocks fucking her. She imagines these young inexperienced men trying their best to live up to expectations they've created in their imaginations. She is surprised by how much concentration it takes for her to purge Stromberg from her cunt.

The dark denims aren't an obvious choice but coupled with the tank and blazer, her outfit is *acceptable*. Her strapless stilettos are almost too high, but just almost. None of the other professors in the staff room are dressed like her. They all look at least their age, and beyond. The formalities of her introduction and orientation are over quicker than she thought, and with a good hour to go before everyone has to be in their first class, they have some time to socialize. Predictably, Mark is on Mariella almost instantly. She can just smile politely.

Despite his picture in the school's prospectus, Mark is not unattractive. It is clear to Mariella why he has his reputation. It wouldn't be too hard to agree to being fucked by the sixty-year-old man. He was fuckable, in an older teacher kind of way. This was a fantasy she had had in her youth and one that she had played out with the very teachers she fantasized about. So there was no unfulfilled need stirring inside her, even now as she finds herself somewhat aroused by the rough-faced man with the accent. She is not about to make him think that she is getting quite wet while listening to him speak. The other teachers, male and female, throw sympathetic looks her way.

"So if there's anything that you need help with, you know where to find me." Mark seems sincere *and flirty*.

"Thank you, sir, I'll be sure to find you, *for anything...*" Mariella takes her flirtation to an elevated level, taking control of the situation from Mark.

"Anything Mariella... and please call me Mark. I wouldn't want my age and experience to be confused unnecessarily." Mark drags the flirtation out a little more.

"There's a difference? ...between age and experience?" Of course, Mariella knows there is.

"There is... a very big difference," His emphasis on 'big' sends a steady beat into Mariella's pussy and she has to excuse herself immediately. Mark knows that he has found his way into parts of her that now leave her open to his advances. So he lets her go, knowing that when the opportunity presents itself, she will be primed.

The class is already half full when she arrives. The enthusiastic first-years sit eagerly at their desks. The veterans trickle in and huddle in familiar groups. Mariella watches the clock on the wall, waiting for it to hit the nine o clock marker before introducing herself. The last five minutes before this happens seem to be the longest of her entire morning. Eventually, though, the class is full and she has to make the dreaded introduction.

"I won't waste time getting each of you to say your names. We'll get to know one another as I grade papers and read through assignments. I'm Miss Garrison, however, and no matter how this year goes, that is the one thing that won't change." Her attempt at a joke goes largely unnoticed.

The rest of the class goes by smoothly. There are a couple of disruptions, all of them from the students who were in the institution last year. Those who're here for the first time are still trying to figure things out. Mariella was clever to get straight into learning, already giving them an assignment that will require them to set up one on one time with her, killing several birds with just one stone. By the time they leave their new professor alone in the class, they all have a pretty good idea of what the rest of the year will be like. The professor herself has little idea of the 150 characters that she will be dealing with, at least not yet.

The smell of her students is still in the room when the door opens and closes. Mark has come to check on her to see how it's gone. He's already discarded his jacket and tie, but his shirt is tucked neatly into his trousers, held up by an expensive and very well chosen belt. As he walks down towards her past the desks, it's obvious by the massive movement in his pants that he isn't wearing underwear. Mariella can't keep her eyes off his cock, watching for every hint of its size. Mark moves to give her the maximum visuals; he gives her exactly what he knows she is watching for.

By the time he is standing behind her reading her class list over her shoulders she already wants to touch it. The problem with wanting it is that she is already aware of what has been said about this man. It's not so much him really, but it's the woman who *warned* her. The idea that she will give in so fast, that she will give in at all, and these women, her colleagues now, would somehow find out about her weakness, seems too much to bear. The door closed also seems to be too much now, it seems obvious and anyone who knew that she was in here with him would get the wrong idea. Mariella really wishes that Mark had left the door open.

"You smell really nice." He has a definite game.

"Thanks." Mariella is irritated that on her first day, and even before, she's been excited by this old guy. She's wondering if it's not just the whole hype that was built up around him and his virility and his bi-sexuality and everything about him that makes him creepy and exotic all at once.

"You've probably heard about me right?" He goes straight for the obvious truth.

"I have," Mariella is glad he has.

"Well just so you know, at my age, I don't sleep with anyone just for the sake of getting laid. I'm old enough to know what I want and I'm not about to waste the massive amounts of sexual energy I have on random fucks with nobodies." Mark goes to the core of what makes him exotic and again he wets Mariella's pussy without even touching it. She suddenly sees him in a very different light, and the moist part of her between her legs is now open to casual fucking with this open-minded, sexually liberated European.

"Let's hope that I'm not considered a *nobody* for very long," She lets him know that she's available.

"We can do something about that right now Miss Garrison. You're everything *but* a nobody!"

"Well thank you, Mark. But it is my first day. Let's give my tender bits a minute to settle in!"

The references made to her vagina harden Mark, and in the absence of underwear, there is no place for his erection to hide. So instead of pretending it isn't there, he points to it and confirms for Mariella that he could fuck her flat across her desk right now. She pulls his attention to the files on her desk and distracts him by getting his opinions on the returning students in her class.

CHAPTER 5

IT'S clear by the end of the week who her problem students are going to be. It's exactly as Mark had predicted. The returning jocks have absolutely no interest in history. Hers is just the easiest class to get into, and also to get out of doing any real work in because it's all mostly group-based assignments. This gives them the freedom to focus on their sports, and then flaunt their jock cocks in her class at the doe-eyed newbies ever eager to do the bulk of their work, all in exchange for the privilege of sucking their cocks. And if said newbies happen to be hot too, they get fucked, *often*.

Three jocks stand out. They are obviously good friends and they've obviously shared more with each other than most boys. At nineteen, they've got the kind of cocks that are ready for action, the kind of dicks that are prone to performing exceptionally well in public. It's obvious from their jokes that they've had several group sessions, and that they do most of their best work together. Their egos feed off of each other, probably in the same way that they do on the football field.

Randy Eckles is the star quarterback. He's old Texas

money and has an attitude and a cock to boot. At ten inches, it isn't huge dick, but it's enough to impress, and to confirm all the good things he tells himself in the mirror every day. John Talley is the team's wide receiver. At six feet he has an impressive fifteen-inch tool. His is the cock that the three-some uses to get group action. He has no problem whipping it out and whirling it around in front of an audience. Brandon Richards, also six feet, is the starting point guard. His cock is an inch bigger than Randy's and is the thickest meat in the trio. Despite the remarkable excess John has, Randy's is the baddest attitude.

Mariella isn't fazed by the attention-seeking youngsters though. She has a set of artillery that she knows will serve her well, provided she approaches the situation with caution. She knows that firstly, they are not doing too well in her class. She also knows that being the star sportsmen that they are, the one thing they thrive on is attention. So her plan is to give them everything but. This is after all *her* class, and the one person who the class is going to be about is Mariella. There is no way that she is going to make all her years at college and her achievement now, junior professor at a prestigious university, about three delinquents who'll probably end up living on food stamps.

Fridays are the easiest for jocks, provided they're not playing a game. And there are no games today. So Randy, John, and Brandon are completely out of control. They spend the bulk of the class planning a party for later and arranging various fucks for the rest of the weekend. The sound of their Blackberries is annoying the rest of the class, especially the new students and the professor, but Mariella is not about to lose her composure. She lets them have the forty-five minutes, knowing that by the time the day is over, they will know that the game has changed. She will play by their rules and show them the implications of taking time from others that isn't theirs to take.

"Randy, John, Brandon?" She times her summons perfectly. With three minutes before the bell, everyone is still seated. And by the time the three are at her desk, and the siren is evicting the rest of the class, it is too late for them to make for the door. They fiddle with the trinkets on her desk without saying a word. Mariella waits too for the class to be empty before she speaks. They think they know what to expect, a reprimand for their behavior, but instead, they're shown a stack of books and asked to follow her.

Without speaking to them, she walks out of the class, exits the building, glides across the courtyard, and then up the stairs to her apartment. She unlocks the door and leaves it open for them to follow. Leaving them with no instruction, they stand with the volumes in hand while she disappears down the hall. She takes her time about whatever she is doing and when she returns they know why. Her soft, formal appearance, the result of a dark-blue suit, has been discarded and replaced with ripped denim cheeky shorts and a soft pick tank. Barefoot, she looks like a first-year student who was a leader of the cheerleading squad in her high school.

"Just drop them on the floor. Thanks, boys." She motions to the floor with her eyes and then picks up her phone, dialing. The three put the books down and then wait, again, watching her, wanting her, needing her to release them. Mariella speaks into the phone.

"Mark, hi. I'm ready for that *thing* you wanted to discuss." She is sure to make sure that her tone is leading, not just to the three men in the room, but to Mark as well, who knows what she is talking about of course but who is a little confused by the ambiguity in her voice.

"That will be all thanks. You guys probably have a weekend to get started." It's obvious that they don't want to leave, and even more obvious that they want to know who Mark is. They take a chance and ask for a drink. Mariella is generous, offering them a seat as well. It takes less than ten minutes for Mark to arrive, in sweat pants and a t-shirt, no underwear. He walks into the room and shakes the boy's hands rigorously, his palms sweaty from his laps around the track, and his cock massive from the cardio workout. It's obvious to all the boys that the sixty-year-old, shorter than all three of them, is sporting a massive dick, probably bigger even than John's. It is, reaching a flaccid length of almost *seventeen* inches.

Mariella has set into motion a game that she knows will at the very least frustrate the shit out of the three who have frustrated her so in her class. She has revealed herself to be as young and desirable as any of the other girls on campus. She has also shown that for all her appeal, she would rather be giving it up to the old dude whose first name they hadn't even known until just now. She lets them finish their drinks, knowing that class is going to be a very different game on Monday. She offers Mark a drink and lets him settle on the tiny balcony, separating them just enough for the three gulping the apple juice in her living room not to hear what they're talking about. She lets their own imaginations drive them completely fucking insane. Every time she leaves them alone to attend to Mark, the three mouth *Stromberg* to each other in disbelief.

Stromberg indeed!

Alone, they take in the breeze, leaving the French doors open so that the entire apartment is privy to the same cool, crisp freshness. They discuss the best approach for the entire year and the faculty that Mariella is now a part of.

The two *work* through a comprehensive lesson plan and manage to cook up a late lunch as well. It's early evening and almost dinner time when Mark is happy that all his years of experience have been sufficiently passed down to his newest mentee. They make their way inside as the air cools down considerably.

"I'm sorry that I came across all sweaty. I didn't expect your call before I'd gotten home." Mark doesn't know how else to delay what seems like an inevitable progression towards the door.

"It's really not a problem. I like the pants," Mariella knows that she pounced the session on him, and they had planned it for after the weekend. But she needed to use him for her little mission, and now she could not in good conscience simply discard the man who had probably, with the help of his freewheeling dick, ensured that she was going to have a much better time in her class. "I'd offer to open a bottle of wine, but since you're uncomfortable in your sweats..." she continues.

"If you show me the bottle, I'll open it myself!" Mark is experienced enough to know an offer to fuck when one is presented to him. Mariella on the other hand knows that she is going to be fucked by him, and this is as good a time as any. She also knows that if she initiates it, then no matter what rumor spreads, she was the one who was the aggressor, making it acceptable to her. She is a powerful woman with a need to occasionally assert this power. She also knows how rumors work and if she comes across as the one who seduced the old man, they both look good, as opposed to her looking weak and easy.

Mark manages to get the bottle open and both glasses filled with the chilled chardonnay before Mariella pulls his pants to his knees. He almost drops his glass but instead takes a big gulp before putting it back on the kitchen table and leaning back against the counter. Mariella takes his cock in her hands and gives it a squeeze and then a pull towards her face. She says nothing as she starts to lick the head, the sweat filling the surface of her tongue with salt. Settling her nose into his soft pubes she takes a whiff, and Mark apologizes again for not showering first.

"Don't be sorry for smelling like a man!" That's all she needs to say.

Mariella takes every part of Mark's cock into her mouth. She doesn't try for the full length of it, that wouldn't be possible. She sucks as far down the fat shaft as she can, letting it sit in her mouth for as long as Mark likes. She allows him to fuck her mouth gently and then leaves the exit up to him. Once he removes his cock from her mouth she bites on the parts of it that did not fit into her mouth. She licks and nibbles until her mouth has attended to every inch. His salty balls seem to be her favorite, Mark apologizing profusely for how he suspects he might taste.

By some miracle of agility, Mariella undresses herself while on her knees and without letting Mark's nuts slip from her tiny mouth. Mark has had his eyes shut the whole time, thoroughly enjoying the kind of aggression in youth seldom found on campus. Everyone he's fucked has for the most part let him lead, assuming this to be a privilege of his age. So when he opens his eyes to see why his dick seems to have been abandoned he is pleasantly surprised to find a naked nymph standing in front of him. Mariella does an about-turn and makes her way to her bed, Mark hot on her heels.

The dark grey sheets are almost masculine. It's obvious that the room is a result of somebody else's efforts, somebody who decorated the room for a man. Mariella climbs onto the bed and summons Mark onto it with her eyes, still clearly visible despite the darkness in the room. Mark reaches for her instead and pulls her back off it. She stands in front of him in anticipation for what he wants to do. It's clear that he isn't going to relinquish *all* control of their fucking. For no reason she can immediately comprehend Mariella takes his left hand in hers and feels for a ring, searching for evidence of such when she finds no band there.

Mark takes her face in his hands and kisses her. The kiss is not what she expects, it's not like the intense linking between flirting and fucking, but an intimate addition to what is essentially a *process*. He kisses her long, he kisses her deeply. Mariella kisses him back, but in response to his kissing because there is nothing that she feels she can add to the perfection of his lips. Mark doesn't stop kissing her even as he sends his thick finger into her vagina. She feels him enter her, but she cannot pull herself from his lips. Mark kisses Mariella for half an hour while bringing her to a delicious orgasm with nothing but his thick index.

Now he lifts her onto the bed. He climbs onto her immediately and follows her as she adjusts herself and positions herself for comfort. Mariella subconsciously finds the same place on her bed where Mark had fucked her in her head on more than one occasion. She realizes also that her imagination had not done this man's dick justice. Mariella points to the side table drawer and inside it, Mark finds a selection of condoms. Fortunately, he finds a super-sized Trojan, his size, and so he suits up his shaft. His mouth is on hers again as he angles his cock and eases it into what is undoubtedly the tightest pussy he's ever had the privilege of enjoying.

The sex is nothing like she'd imagined. Mark is not his

age. Or maybe he is. He doesn't need any gimmicks, no tricks required. He uses nothing but his generous cock to bring the young and not entirely inexperienced Mariella to orgasm after orgasm. He fucks her hard and then makes the gentlest love to her. He moves her around on the bed, positioning and repositioning her to make every stroke, every round, every session a completely mind-blowing experience. Mariella breaks into several sweats way before he does, and even when Mark finally shoots his last load, his brow is just slightly moist.

There are absolutely no regrets when she wakes up the next day to find that the *old pervert* hasn't left. She doesn't care that he will probably be seen leaving her flat too early for someone who's just popped in for a coffee on a Sunday morning. They fuck for the better part of the morning and then do something even more unexpected; they talk through lunch. There is nothing romantic or leading about the conversation. It is the mature banter of two consenting adults who've absolutely enjoyed fucking each other. Whatever Mark's reputation, they should definitely add *super-skilled fucker* to it. She finds, as she lets him go, walking with him all the way to his car, that for this kind of sex, she couldn't give a fuck what reputation she earns around campus.

CHAPTER 6

IT'S NOT ENTIRELY unexpected that the three most inconspicuous students in her class on this perfect Monday morning are John, Randy, and Brandon. They are only inconspicuous in that they are not their usual trouble-causing selves. Instead today they watch every move that Mariella makes, undressing her easily since she has decided to play it incredibly casual and wear a knee-length summer frock and beach thongs. She has obviously settled into herself within the context of this institution, not making the conservative environment alter or suppress the beach girl that she is. John, Randy, and Brandon don't move even after the bell has gone and the class has emptied.

"Can I help you, boys?" She asks when it's clear that they're going nowhere.

"You could miss, or we could help you!" They don't speak together but they may as well be.

"Are we going to cross a line here gentlemen?" She plays the teacher.

"No ma'am, not unless you want us to!" They're cocky

alright, and it's obvious that under their desks their hands are on what must be their incredibly hard cocks.

"Would we be talking about the same line here that Mr. Stromberg so skillfully crossed all weekend?" She knows just how to break their fragile juvenile egos.

"The dude's a dinosaur. You might be pleasantly surprised by what is possible for your fine self in *this* century, ma'am." Randy's attitude and arrogance take their place front and center.

"Well, why don't you boys look me up when you're a little less like attention-seeking *Chihuahuas*, and a whole lot more like **T-Rex**!" She leaves them to their cocks and fantasies and walks out of the room.

It's obvious for the rest of the week that the three have a hard time processing the Chihuahua reference. They're dogs alright; But not that kind of dog. And it seems to be getting ever more obvious that Miss Garrison doesn't give a flying fuck about what kind they are actually. She's fucking a T-Rex, and not in the fossil-find kind of way, but in the king of all beasts that have ever walked the earth kind of way. Mark Stromberg is old. But now the three youngsters have had to look at the man differently, objectively. And this objective look reveals Prof Strom to be a very attractive, decently built, highly virile, excessively dicked *MAN!*

The situation is almost too incomprehensible to the three jocks.

They're given their task of carrying the 150 assignment folders to Mariella's flat again. The walk is not so quiet this time, the three dropping hint after hint as to how they can do a much better job of satisfying the young Mariella. They emphasize her youth repeatedly. She loves it. She also loves the fact that Mark has proven to be every bit a man worthy of envy. What she knows though is that the three will soon become bored with wanting her and return to their old taunts when they know that they can't have her. They fell fast for her farce, and are now putty in her hands. It won't last though if she doesn't keep their desire for her peaked.

The circumstance is frustrated by the fact that the three are in their final year. This is their second attempt at the Introduction To History course, and you don't get a third. They'll have to find another softer academic course next year if they fail. So they know that she won't have anything to do with them after this year. What this means for them is that if they don't get to prove themselves to her, the opportunity will be lost. What this means for Mariella is that if she cannot keep them hoping, wanting, and yearning for the duration of the year, they will punish her by making her class impossible to teach. She could just hand them over to Mark, or another senior official, but her age makes this seem inappropriate somehow.

Mark will discipline them, however, just not in the way he normally would in the stringent walls of his office. This isn't going to be a strong verbal reprimand with threats of expulsion or bans from sports games. It's going to be the worst kind of reprimand for their young impressionable minds. He walks in barely a minute after Mariella and the jocks. It's Mark this time who asks them if they want juice *or something*. Mark makes conversation with them about their plans for the weekend and their plans with their girl-friends. He deliberately lingers on their physical abilities with women and makes comparisons with himself, suggesting that if he was a few years younger... They can't take it.

Mariella walks out with a pitcher of ice tea and suggests that the young men in the room sort themselves out. A minute later she hands a chilled bottle of chardonnay to

Mark and holds out the glasses for him to pour. It's obvious that as soon as they leave, Mark and Mariella will be in a whole other mood, edged on by wine and their attractiveness. The thought that there will be some decent fucking happening in this space shortly goes straight to their dicks, and immediately John, Randy, and Brandon regret the pants they wear. Their erections are obvious. Very obvious! Mark is the first to spot them, not entirely because he hasn't been throwing a *bi-eye* in the general direction of their crotches.

"Getting a little hot there boys?" He teases. Mariella sees what he is looking at. She smiles to herself and pretends not to have seen. But then she catches Mark's face and they are suddenly on the same page. They say everything that they need to with their eyes and the game is suddenly on.

They both know that it will be incredibly embarrassing to let them out now, their cocks too much, and therefore too visible. This does present the opportunity though for the discipline that only the man that is Mark will understand. And by the look on Mariella's face, she will play along. They get up and walk towards the bedroom, wine in hand, without saying a word. Then just before they disappear down the hall Mark turns around and says to them, "Let yourselves out when you're ready gents."

There's a moment of preparation that Mariella and Mark get through in seconds without speaking. They draw the dark curtains completely and re-angle the bed with the stealth of military personnel, *silently*. They leave the door ajar just enough for the three to be able to see into the darkness without having to push the door anymore. Fortunately for the three curious minds, already walking towards the door, the hallway is as dark as the room, so there is no risk of any shadowy giveaways. The benefit to the two drinking chardonnay in the dark is that the darkness will deter the boys from attempting to use cell phones to record what's about to go down. The red lights will be too obvious in the black.

Mariella and Mark speak to each other in whispers for the time it takes for them to finish the bottle of wine. They wait for the telltale sounds of feet trying not to make contact with the wooden floor. It's a mission impossible. As soon as they are obviously in position, leaning against the frame of the door and straining to see into the room, Mark takes over as the master of ceremonies. Both he and Mariella are comfortable in the knowledge that all that is visible from the door are their shadows. So they'll need to make it an absolutely athletic performance to give the boys as clear an idea of what is going down as possible.

For the next hour, Mark takes Mariella on a journey that has her forget in minutes that there are three men in her hallway wanting to see her getting fucked. He proves in the invisibility of the room that John, Randy, and Brandon combined have got a hell of a lot to learn before they think that they can even begin to satisfy a woman the way Mark is obviously satisfying Mariella. They have never heard a woman make the sounds that she is making, they have never smelt a woman's pussy emit so powerful scent. She is obviously incredibly aroused. And Mark obviously knows exactly what to do with her arousal.

They can only take it for another half an hour before they make it for the outside of the flat. They stand in the foyer for a minute so as to allow their erections to subside. They head straight for their dorm and get stuck into chilled cans of beer and fiery porn, beating their meat over and over again, watching women that aren't Mariella being fucked every which way. But each time they shoot a load they close their eyes and imagine the young professor whose pussy is currently being split by a fossil. All of them force the fossil imagery just to placate their egos, but they know that he is very much their senior in the lovemaking department.

Back in Mariella's apartment, another bottle of wine is opened by a naked pair. They take it right back to the room and crack a window, repositioning the bed and opening the door completely now that they know that the front door is locked. They chat and joke about the three men who have been having the wickedest thoughts about *ma'am*. The wine goes down smoothly and quenches every thirst except one. It becomes ever clearer that they have a desire for each other that touches every part of their physical selves. It's not an emotional wanting. Mark and Mariella are just highly compatible sexually, their open-mindedness a definite factor.

With the taste of chardonnay on his lips and the smell of it on his breath, Mark dives into Mariella's vagina. Because of all the men who've gone down on her before, Mariella expects a licking, or maybe a sucking. She expects that maybe he might bite into her pussy or fuck her hole with his tongue. Mark Stromberg does none of these things. He does the one thing that Mariella doesn't expect. He takes a very deep breath and *blows very, very gently all over the entire surface of her vagina.*

Every inhalation seems deeper because every time Mark blows back onto her pussy he lingers longer. Every time he blows onto her it's harder and more intense, ending in a soft waft of warm air in just the right spots. He does this over and over again, and each time he brings Mariella closer to climax, but also raises inside her a burning desire to have his massive dick inside her. But Mark makes no move to fuck her. He takes each of her thighs firmly in hand and just keeps on blowing her. No part of his mouth makes contact with her pussy, just his breath. He reaches a momentum and establishes a rhythm from which there is no reverse.

Mariella wants to scream. She does. She silences herself with a pillow. It does nothing but muffle the sounds escaping her. She screams over and over into the pillow begging for Mark to just fuck her. He doesn't. He blows harder and harder. Then he blows agonizingly softly. There is no way for Mariella to get her cunt to make contact with any part of Mark and he knows this. And then, just when she feels she is about to die as if she is going to explode into a million frustrated pieces, Mark envelopes her pussy with his mouth, shoots his tongue into her, and rapidly licks the inside of her cunt deep and hard until she does explode, shooting a very satisfied load into Mark's very satisfying mouth.

CHAPTER 7

"SO IT'S obvious that they want to fuck you!" Mark says as he exits the shower. They laugh about the possibility of it and for a minute they entertain the *how* of it. The thing about being a mature fuck buddy is that you get to discuss other possibilities with each other without it being awkward. The narcissistic pair decides that this might actually be just the thing to unequivocally dethrone the threesome. If they are now given the opportunity to actually fuck Mariella, and it ends with less than an explosion, then they will be too shy to try any further tricks in her class.

It's clear though to both Mariella and Mark that the possibility of them actually doing anything in Mariella's class that she actually *can't* handle is a big zero. So now it really is just a curious game that they've decided to play for the fun of it. Why not give the arrogant kids a final year to remember? Why not humble them so that they never again approach any pussy with arrogance? Mariella and Mark see this as a favor that they're doing to whoever happens to find themselves under John, Randy, or Brandon outside of this university at any time in the future.

After Mark leaves Mariella is left to think of the fun she will have with her jocks. She doesn't for a second consider that they might deny her, the thought absurd. Alone, she starts to imagine what power hides in the pants of the men who taunted her in her first few weeks. Now they fawn over her, following her not like love-struck puppies, but like lust-struck beasts. And now she has resolved to tame these beasts, not entirely unselfishly, of course, her cunt excited by the possibility of a youthful penis. Experienced dick is better, however, but the inexperience of youth is always *interesting*.

Not surprisingly, Mark just wants the story after. He has no interest in taped sessions for amusement in the privacy of his bedroom. This destroys once and for all the perverted reputation that those who've been fucked and discarded by Mark have given him around campus. It is now clear to Mariella that he is just a fun-loving, sexually evolved being who probably gets bored easily once an escapade gets *clingy*. She makes a mental note to end it on a high, but never to end it without the possibility of an occasional revisit. But this isn't something with which to occupy her mind right now. Right now, she has to figure out who is going to be first to stray into *Pandora's Box*.

The week is filled with ever shorter dresses and a variety of exotic scents that she makes sure John, Randy, and Brandon get a whiff of before they leave. She becomes very mobile in her class, often leaving the board empty and parading herself between her students, creating an intimate setting in which all her students are suddenly very comfortable with her. The boys though, three, in particular, are anything but comfortable. Mariella knows that they are clever enough for her game to be obvious. So this means that none of them will be trapped. They will play willingly into her hands.

It's Thursday before the first man falls. It's not Randy, whose arrogance would have made him the obvious candidate. At the top of the stairs leading to her apartment is a very edgy Brandon. He has a cheeky look in his innocent almond eyes, a smile on his face. But his hands move nervously over each other and his feet are not able to stay on the tiled floor for longer than a minute at a time. By the time Mariella is standing in front of him though he seems to have gathered himself enough to revert to full jock mode.

"It's not fair you know, what you've been doing to us over the last while..." He keeps biting on his bottom lip in an effort to look composed and deliberately sexy. It's unnecessary though because the boy is fucking hot.

"And what exactly have I been doing to you, besides teaching you a history class?!"

"Oh, you know ma'am. First making yourself all fresh and hot, and then giving it up to old man Stromberg. And then making is so we find out. And then getting sexier and sexier every day so that we can't take it anymore and now I'm standing here not sure if I'm not just making a complete fool of myself." There is something mature about Brandon suddenly and Mariella finds herself inviting him in before confirming in her head that Brandon is going to be lucky number one.

Inside her apartment, she offers him a glass of ice tea. He asks for a glass of wine instead. They laugh at his boldness.

"Drinking my wine isn't a guarantee that you'll get to sip from my vine..." Mariella speaks with a lowered husk that has Brandon hard instantly. He accepts the tea and sits on the sofa so as to hide his erection. She's already seen it and goes over to lock the door before pouring herself a glass of wine. Brandon watches her sip from the glass in silence.

Mariella positions herself in front of him and asks him to empty his pockets. She checks that there is not a private recording being made that will amuse his friends later, or be used against her if he should need leverage for better grades. With his phone on her sofa next to him turned off, she lifts her dress, revealing perfectly pink panties with Thursday written across her cunt in yellow ladybirds. Brandon doesn't know whether to take off his own pants or pull down her panties. Her panties win, her vagina suddenly the only thing he wants to see.

Mariella steps out of her undies and lifts her dress over her shoulders at the same time. Brandon wants to sniff her panties but knows this to be an old porn cliché. He drops them next to his phone. Standing up now, he also removes his clothes, his boxers getting caught briefly on his solid erection. He has a perfectly shaped penis and all she wants to do is suck it. But sucking on his dick will give him the illusion that she wants him as badly as he wants her. So instead she steps back away from him and gives him a '*this is me, now what*' look. He takes a very deep breath and then proceeds to show her just what!

His hands are on each of her breasts and he gives them gentle squeezes. He watches her face as he touches her tits, licks, and then sucks her nipples, and then returns to squeezing them. Slowly she warms to his fingers and moves a little closer to him. Brandon's hands move down over her torso and rest on her waist. He lets his fingers dance on her midriff, giving her perfection the appreciation it deserves. He circles her naval with his index for the longest time before getting onto his knees in front of her and easing her legs apart. Brandon takes another deep breath at the breathtaking visuals of his professor's pussy.

Her ass becomes the resting place for his fingers as he pulls her pussy towards his face. Mariella almost expects him to blow, but instead, his tongue sends instant sprites of fire onto her clit. She wishes he was slower about starting, but soon his pace is perfect. She surprises herself by how quickly he has managed to arouse her but then remembers that the way kids are fucking today, it's never a long drawn-out affair. They need to squeeze it into a couple of minutes at parties or behind the bleachers during training. So while they've not mastered the art of lovemaking, they are experts at the quickie. Brandon has managed to arouse her enough for her not to need him to slow down though.

He pulls his jeans off the sofa and fumbles for a condom, leaving Mariella's pussy unattended. She watches as he wraps his dick in the sheath and then gives it a stroke so that it swells and fills the plastic totally. He tugs on his own balls as he again finds her clit with his tongue, leaving her this time to find her own balance. Jocks really are very selfish about fucking, but with a dick like his, who the fuck cared. If there was one thing that Mariella had told herself, it was that no matter how these boys fucked her, she would not be left wanting an orgasm. Regardless of the fact that they would leave thinking they hadn't impressed her much, she would not stand for her pussy being left yearning.

She allows him to suck on her cunt and lick the inside of her vagina long enough for her to get so close to cumming that even if Brandon managed just five strokes inside her cunt it would be enough for her to blow. He doesn't stop though and brings her to a total orgasm with his tongue. She makes a mental note of her satisfaction and then allows him to suck up to her climax without showing too much excitement. She finds her wine and takes a sip, offering him more ice tea while he pulls ever harder on his balls. He gives a quizzical look, allows her one more sip, and then pulls her back towards himself. He sits on the sofa and then pulls her legs astride him before easing her down.

Brandon holds his cock up as he settles Mariella over it, and then on to it. He reclines into the sofa as his cock disappears completely into her. With his head on the backrest and his feet firmly on the floor, he pushes Mariella away from him and then pulls her back towards himself. He adds to this movement an upward thrusting so that the drag on his cock is coupled with an equal drag on her cunt. He is not going to assume that she is going to enthusiastically ride the shit out of his cock, and so he is going to simply do his best to create the illusion that this is happening.

His skill is obvious. Mariella is in total heaven being in the controlling hands of the footballer. She doesn't pretend to be bored but manages to contain her excitement to the extent that she has two orgasms without Brandon noticing. He picks up only on the fact that every so often her pussy tightens considerably around his dick. What this does is encourage him to thrust harder into her and therefore by default send her into climax. She has four orgasms before she allows him to see her progression towards one. This is going to be the final, it just has to be. She had thought that he would be so excited that he would cum in minutes, but he's proven himself up to the task. Of course, he employed the age-old 'wank a few times before you show up, so there was no urgency to cum at all' strategy that any jock with a reputation to uphold would be aware of.

But once he felt he had her well on her way to orgasm, he started to fuck her with his cock in mind. He hit harder and deeper and soon he too was on his way home. She can't hide from him that the fact that he manages to hold himself back until she blows before letting himself shoot is impressive. But his ego stroke is short-lived when she gets up, gets dressed, and gives him a *'hurry up and leave'* look. He did expect a little aftercare but she's obviously not going to be giving him any. She picks up her phone and confirms an appointment with Mark before turning to Brandon who is fumbling with his jeans,

"This isn't something we need to be telling anybody now is it Brandon?! After all, it's not like the earth moved or nothing!" She rushes in the direction of the bathroom while a shattered Brandon leaves in shame.

CHAPTER 8

JOHN AND RANDY all but flip a coin for the next attempt. But Brandon finally lets them know how his tryst actually ended and so they decide that it would boil down to a question of cock. Randy has about four or five inches less meat than John, and John has less than Mark. So they decide that Randy should go next, so that if he too doesn't deliver and have her screaming for more than John could redeem the entire jock fraternity just by sheer size and strength. John will therefore be their last attempt to save face.

So, Randy, it is!

The three make absolutely certain that Randy is the only one available to carry the assignments to Mariella's flat on this particular Friday. It's been a day since Brandon's 'failure', and they decide to strike while the iron is hot. They reason that at the very least her curiosity will have been sparked and she might want to check to see if it could possibly get any worse. Randy wears shorts to show his thick legs and no underwear so as to create the perfect awkward moment that will either lead to fucking, or expose his dick unnecessarily to his history professor. She already knows that he's going to get everything that he wants, and then some.

Inside her flat she watches him put the folders on the table. She watches him pull unnecessarily on his shorts, adjusting them so that the tip of his cock hangs past the hem. His erection points south deliberately and she wonders briefly if he thinks she's going to drop to her knees, open her mouth and save it from falling to the floor. She stares at his meat and then finds his eyes. She says nothing and waits for him to explain why she now has his exposed penis in her living room. He is silent and suddenly looks confused and nervous. She smiles only to herself.

"I take it Brandon spoke to you." She makes him seem obvious.

Randy stutters for a minute and then, "yes ma'am, he did. Says you were everything he dreamed you'd be."

"And now you want to see if I can be everything you dreamed?" She looks at his dick as she speaks.

"Yes ma'am, please ma'am." He replies.

Mariella laughs at his honesty.

Something about her laugh has Randy assume that she wants him to remove his clothes because this is exactly what he does. She lets him stand naked for a minute in front of her, just long enough for him to start to feel awkward. He covers his dick with both hands as soon as his insecurities have him lose his hard-on. She then removes her clothing slowly, immediately reviving his erection so that his hands can no longer contain his meat. Naked now too, Mariella walks toward Randy with aggression that has him step back a bit.

The jock from her class is suddenly gone. He is transformed by his awkwardness into a cute young man about to lose his virginity. Mariella wishes for a moment that she had underplayed it a bit so that arrogant Randy stood in front of her now. But she has ways of bringing that bastard to the surface. So she enjoys watching him squirm for a little while longer. Mariella stands and stares at his cock as it hardens more and jerks involuntarily to the side in anticipation of what stands in front of him.

Finally, she reaches for him and runs her fingers along his hairy abdomen. His rippled torso is impressive. Mariella's fingers find his pubes and then pass his cock to cup his nut sack. As soon as she lands on the hot balls Randy is fired up again. He is no longer shy as her fingers on him confirm for him that she wants him. Randy thrives on being wanted. He loves being desired. This makes him suddenly more intent on making himself desirable, irresistible almost. He needs her to want only him, and once she has had him, he wants Mariella to know unequivocally that he is the best she's ever had. Randy needs to be the best.

He bites into her neck and lifts her off the ground. Randy carries Mariella easily, and she sits in his hands as they cup her ass. She hangs her arms around his neck but this is not necessary to keep her up. Randy continues to nibble her neck, biting harder and then not. He rubs his face against hers but makes no attempt to kiss her. Suddenly kissing him is something she desires, probably because of his continuous hinting at this. But she won't lose herself to him. This is her show.

When Randy realizes eventually that while he has obviously turned her on, his finger checking her pussy occasionally, finding it wet, that he is not going to get her lips, and that this is going to be the usual type of *I am man* fucking he and his buddies are accustomed to, he forms a strategy in his head. He is going to need to put a lot more effort into satisfying this woman, who has a little more experience than the girls they usually fuck. So he needs to think of a different strategy, one that he hopes will be well received by Mariella, who clearly has her own strategy in play.

The closest available surface is the small dining table. Randy sits her down on it and then pushes her down on to her back. He pulls her so that his cock has access to her cunt, and he hits his heavy dick repeatedly onto her clit. This sends shots of pressure into her. But instead of moaning, she giggles. Randy doesn't expect this and suddenly wants to just ram his rod into her and show her that he's a man. He hates the sound of her laughter in the circumstance, despite this being the same giggle that turned him on so many times in class.

Instead of his cock though, Randy shoots a finger into her. He fills her cunt quickly with three fingers and fucks her with them fast. Mariella holds on to the table and spreads her legs apart, begging him to go harder, to go faster, to go deeper. He's already hitting her spot but he doesn't need to know this. Randy holds her legs as wide as he can now with one hand and really gives her pussy a good dig. Again she is able to have an orgasm without giving too much away. All he knows is that her pussy is moister than it was when he started digging.

With her cunt wet Randy sends his cock into her before she knows it. The surprise has her sit up to check that he has in fact entered her. His cock feels remarkable inside her. As she surveys her cunt, Randy doesn't move, allowing her to take it all in. Once she settles back down onto her back Randy starts fucking her hard. He fucks her deep and intensely while fingering her clit rapidly. Mariella holds tightly onto the table, her head trying hard to contain her body as Randy delivers the most intense fucking pleasure, really giving her cunt a fantastic run. She can't contain it. She explodes, a loud scream escaping from her mouth as Randy brings her to a brilliant orgasm. Randy knows he's done a decent job.

It takes Mariella less than a minute to pull Randy off the pedestal he's obviously mounted as he strokes his cock proudly. She watches him for a while and then pours them both a glass of wine. Then she picks up Randy's phone and hands it to him.

"Do you want to maybe check what John is doing?" She lets the expression on her face confirm that she means exactly what Randy thinks she means.

It's not that Randy isn't thrown by this. It's not that he isn't offended slightly. It's not that he doesn't wish that he had been able to completely satisfy the absolutely perfect cunt that was his to satisfy. But Randy, John, and Brandon have always been a formidable tag team. They have been a team of powerful cocks that have left multiple pussies satisfied all across campus. Together they have triple-fucked singles and also been at times the only three cocks in a room of as many as twelve women. So together, they will stand a much better chance of taming the fiery Mariella, this woman who seems to so easily pull from them whatever self-confidence the three had spent years thinking that they had.

John arrives with Brandon in tow, an addition suggested via text from Randy and unknown to Mariella until they are at her door. It's her turn to be taken aback, but she lets the two in and turns to Randy, the look on her face saying *touché*. It's clear that the three are on to her now, and that they are desperate to salvage some of their reputations. They've built up to this moment in class so often with taunts and jokes, hints and suggestions, and now, all but

John have left Mariella *wanting*. But Mariella has her own final trump, and she disappears into her bedroom alone.

By the time she has returned to her living room, Mariella has sent a text of her own. She has invited Mark to join them for a little exhibition. He would be arriving in about an hour. Mariella finds that the three have helped themselves to her wine cabinet. They try to look as relaxed as possible, but it is clear that they are relying on the wine to relax them. All of them are naked, and Mariella is impressed by what she sees between John's legs. She needs to give him a solo run before Mark arrives. Once Stromberg gets here she is going to give the three a grand display of what it is to be made love to, and what it looks like to be fucked.

John pulls her to him and sits her next to him on the couch. Randy stands in front of them and Brandon sits on the other side of Mariella so that she is between him and John. Brandon is on her breasts, touching them, rubbing them, and tugging on her nipples. John parts her legs and feels gently over her cunt, not digging into it yet, but hinting at penetration with his fingers. Randy comes to her face with his cock so that before she can think about it she is opening her mouth and his penis is sliding into it. John and Brandon need to stop what they're doing now because the show is a super hot one. They watch as Mariella pulls on Randy's balls while he fucks her mouth until he squirms, whimpers, and then cums in her mouth almost too quickly. The other two laugh at him.

Randy is already pulling another erection from himself while Brandon finally gets his cock into Mariella's mouth. He had wanted nothing more the last time he was here, and now that it's happening, it's too much for him. She sucks on his dick hard as he thrusts into her, and just like Randy, he shoots a load into her too soon. She consoles him by licking the head of his dick and then sucking on his balls. By the time she is done with him, he already has another erection, and he joins Randy in stroking his own cock and keeping his erection firm while John takes over and for the first time has Mariella all to himself.

John has no desire it seems to be sucked. He makes no movement to encourage this. Mariella is glad because her jaw needs a bit of a break. What he does have her do though is sucked hard on his nuts while he puts on a condom. He begs her almost, to bite harder and harder into his nuts. She obliges him, and even while she thinks she's hurting him, he obviously loves it. Once he rolls the condom all the way down his massive shaft he leaves her biting for a little bit more while he spits his palm and masturbates hard. He has a very aggressive stroke. Mariella hopes that his fucking will be the same.

There are minutes left before Mark is due to arrive. The last thing she wants is for him to interrupt John. He seems to sense her desire for him and lifts her off the ground. He puts her in front of the sofa and bends her over. Randy and Brandon are seated on the couch pulling on their cocks and reaching for and touching her breasts. They send fingers into her mouth and then pull on their cocks harder. Mariella comes down occasionally and sucks on the two cocks that are miles from another orgasm so both men just enjoy her mouth. John hits his cock onto her ass cheeks over and over again and then rubs it against her clit. He pushes his dick hard against her pussy in mock thrusts and then gets down to give her hole a good slobbering with his tongue.

Mariella gasps when John finally digs his dick into her pussy as he pushes it slowly into her. It's everything she had imagined, as the over-enthusiastic, oversized penis immediately starts to shred her cunt just as soon as it is all the way inside her. John fucks Mariella so hard that she can concentrate on nothing else and so Randy and Brandon have to take full control of their meat. They manage to get to another orgasm motivated most by the sounds of John annihilating Mariella's pussy. They angle themselves so that they have an optimal view, and despite having just cum, they maintain rock solid erections. It takes an over-zealous John fifteen minutes to shoot his load, in which time he's managed to give Mariella two intense orgasms.

He's just removed his condom when the doorbell rings. The three jocks look at each other to their clothes. Mariella urges them to relax and sort out their condoms before popping another bottle or two. She throws a robe on and goes to the door. The sound of Mark Stromberg has all three empty their glasses twice by the time he is standing in the living room sizing them up. They stutter for a minute but as soon as he starts to get undressed they relax a little more. But as soon as the sixty-year-old is completely naked in front of them, he pulls all their insecurities to the surface again as he quickly achieves a full erection that looks easily like twenty thick inches. It's actually just over 17 inches of thick cock but insecurity has a way of exaggerating perceptions. Mariella lets them soak it in before joining Mark in the center of the room and telling them to relax.

Mariella orders four pizzas and a couple of six-packs while Mark makes sure that there will be a steady supply of chilled wine. John singlehandedly brings the mattress from the bedroom while Randy and Brandon shift things around in the living room so that the king-size mattress can fit in the compact space. It takes less than an hour for everyone to be settled and for all the deliveries to arrive. Mariella manages a lavender and vanilla shower to prepare herself for Mark and his expertise. She enters the space naked and slightly dripping, and finds the men chatting casually about Mark's fitness routine and the various cultures across the world that have a tradition of penis enlargement. Another hour passes and everyone is fed and tipsy.

Mark lays Mariella on the mattress and positions her so that no matter what he does to her, or she to him, there will never be an awkward view. The audience members make themselves comfortable on both sofa and cushions on the floor, each of them rocking a chilled six-pack and a hard-on. There is no need to make any grand announcements once the candles are lit and the lights are turned off completely. Everyone settles into what was originally meant as a showy display of expert lovemaking but is now an intimate lesson from a master to humble, eager students.

Her legs are stretched out and slightly parted. Mark's fingers flutter all over her and immediately Mariella moans, the response so authentic that John, Randy, and Brandon move closer to her. They gather around her head and shoulders and after checking with Mark that they won't be in the way, watch on as Stromberg proceeds. Mark makes very slow work of massaging imaginary oils into the supple parts of Mariella and digging slightly harder into the firmer parts. Every time he resumes the fluttering of his fingers she is again moaning loudly at his touch. This amazes the three who have always thought that harder and faster was always better.

When Mark brings Mariella to an orgasm by simply blowing onto her vagina, the onlookers are floored. They roar and high-five each other while patting Mark on the back, surprising him. Everyone bursts out laughing and everyone has a quick drink before Mariella is served up as the next course. Without any further speaking, Mark turns her onto her side and positions himself behind her. He lifts her leg and pulls it back over his so that the others, who are now in front of a reclined Mariella, can watch as he pinches and pulls on her clit while gliding into her with his solid manhood.

There is something about how Mark moves inside Mariella that is itself a spectacle. He settles his meat inside her and then instead of moving back and forth, he moves Mariella over his cock. He sends his hand under her thigh and keeps her legs apart while applying just enough pressure on her for her to tense and relax enough for the movement of cock over cunt to be obvious. As soon as he brings her close to another orgasm he starts to put his back into it. He starts to add his own thrusting to Mariella's movements now and the show picks up in intensity. He gives a few more tugs to her clit before releasing it completely and proceeding with an hour of absolutely mind-blowing fucking.

The two traverse the length and breadth of the mattress and occasionally roll onto the floor. Everyone moves with them and completely forgets themselves as Mark and Mariella completely wrap themselves in one another now. The lesson has somehow ended for Mark and he takes his entire focus and shifts it to satisfying Mariella. This is another surprise for the three boys watching and when after a further three hours Mark has yet to shoot and Mariella has had a thousand very audible orgasms, it all makes sense to them. They understand not only that they can if they choose get better and better at lovemaking with age, but also that you don't need to cum all the time. Climax for a man doesn't need to be the destination. Once it is clear on their faces that every lesson has been learned, and once Mark gets confirmation from Mariella of complete and total satisfaction, he brings himself to a steady climax in about twenty minutes of intense fucking. Both he and Mariella fall into each other in a sweaty heated heap and their watchers attend to them with drinks and an almost unacceptable but very enjoyable cigarette.

John, Randy, and Brandon spend the rest of the year working very closely with their professors to bring up their grades, and by the time they graduate they've done very well. The sex has been awesome too, and thanks to Mark Stromberg's mentorship, they will make the most attentive lovers to every woman, and the odd man they come into contact with sexually hence. Mark and Mariella develop an ever-increasingly adventurous relationship and by the time Mark Stromberg retires from the University, he is Mariella's husband. They continue to have an incredibly satisfying sex life.

INSURANCE AGENT ALL-STAR

The trouble with being in the insurance business in Los Angeles is that if you're a woman, and a Latina woman at that, you will be paying corrupt officials daily just to stay in business. It doesn't help Zarita Ordonez much that her staff is made up entirely of Latin immigrants, not entirely by accident. The Latino community had a habit of supporting its own, and so with the growing community in the greater Los Angeles area, it just made sense to dress her business with people who not only needed the work but who would bring in the money.

To say that Zarita was doing well was an understatement. She did so well that she was attracting all the wrong kinds of attention from officials. They didn't care to support her much and keep her in business. They just cared that she stayed in business because that meant that she could keep lining their pockets every time they threatened her with Immigration Services or the IRS. Her papers, and her staff's, were all in order mind you. But there was still no better leverage, real or fabricated, that you could hold over a non-citizen. Still, Zarita, motivated by her desire to do good for her little girl Nina, pressed on and made her business work.

If there is one thing that can keep even the hardest working woman's stress in check, it's a man with a powerful cock and the ability to use it. Fortunately for the sexy thirty-five-year-old boss lady, one of her first hires, an ex-trucker turned insurance salesman all-star who's been with her for three years already, is just this man. Santiago Sanchez is almost forty and looks it. His life has been a hard one and it shows in every line on his face. But through the lines and the working past, he has adapted well to his new life in America. Also, Santiago is incredibly handsome, with deep-set mysterious eyes that make *all* his flaws negligible.

They always wait for Nina to be asleep before Santiago comes over. And it's usually on days like today when threats of fabricated charges that might lead to deportation have left Zarita poorer by thousands of dollars that she needs what Santiago has to offer. What the two of them have is not a relationship. It's not even a sexual arrangement of conve-nience. They are close friends who have an intimate under-standing of the dynamics of their predicament. Santiago and Zarita are friends with every kind of benefit. It's been like this almost since day one.

Santiago comes in the back as always, the door left unlocked. He secures it and navigates the kitchen without turning on the lights. He knows this house well. The light from the top of the staircase guides his steps so that he doesn't stumble on his way up and possibly wake Nina. They don't want to confuse the girl in any way so as far as she is concerned, Uncle Santiago works with mom at her office, that's all. Santiago removes his shoes once on the landing and slides down the hall in his socks, silently.

Zarita is already naked on her bed. The light catches

every one of her perfect curves. Santiago closes the door softly and locks it. They speak in whispers as he removes his socks, then his watch. He empties his pockets and puts the contents on the side table. Sitting on the bed he removes his pants, then his boxers. Finally, his sweatshirt comes off and he relaxes against the many pillows. Zarita moves up close to him and throws her arms over his excessively hairy body. Santiago really has a lot of hair everywhere. But his raven curls are deliciously soft.

While sipping on a full-bodied red they discuss, still in whispers, the shakedown they got again today. The interrogations were becoming so predictable that they didn't really pay them too much mind. But with the amount of money that Zarita had to pay in bribes to the corrupt bastard threatening to fabricate sufficient evidence to get her deported and her operation shut down, it was a little more than annoying. It was already costing her so much just to stay in business, what with all the extra costs, so on days like today especially she needed the distraction that Santiago had always been able to offer.

Her hands run up and down his leg, focused on his thigh. This warms his cock but doesn't harden it immediately. Santiago closes his eyes because he knows what is about to happen. He knows not to interrupt Zarita now as she begins to use him for her own pleasure, something that he absolutely loves. He parts his legs as she makes her way between them, moving himself closer to the middle of the bed so that they are both comfortable, and safe from falling. Zarita lifts his balls out of the way and gives hard licks to the space between his ass and his nuts. Santiago is rock hard in an instant.

She takes his balls in her mouth and uses her saliva to warm his orbs. She strokes his cock for a while and then runs her tongue up it until her lips are on his head. He watches his cock disappear into her mouth, her fingers finding and digging into the part under his nuts that her tongue had found first. This sends Santiago into a blissful state that has him moan and shut his eyes often, although he keeps checking the action on his cock, Zarita's mouth a beautiful sight as it negotiates his bent dick.

Santiago reaches down and parts Zarita's ass. He wets his finger in her mouth and then finds her hole with it. He takes a bit of strain bending over her to get to her hole. They move to reposition themselves so that while Zarita keeps sucking, her ass is face up on his chest, giving him access to both her holes comfortably now. Santiago wets his fingers again and digs not just into her ass now, but also into her pussy. He fingers her holes gently and deeply so that they warm up and relax with each movement, and so that her pussy heats up and moistens. He needs to get her ready for his cock because when she is as stressed as she was today, she likes to be fucked hard.

He progresses from gentle fingering to a more intense intrusive style. He digs into her pussy now with opposite indexes and pushes against her inner walls, forcing the entrance to her vagina wider and wider apart. Zarita's scent overwhelms Santiago now and he releases her cunt from his fingers, takes his hands and holds them under her thighs, and pulls her firmly up to his mouth, removing her mouth from most of his cock. Zarita is grateful that she can at least still get his head in her mouth. She really loves the process of sucking on him and also just enjoys the simple taste of him.

Santiago drinks eagerly from Zarita's cunt. The loudest thing in the room is their breathing now as both of them get to the point where all conversation is forgotten and they become all about the business of fucking. Sucking into Zarita's vagina sends pulse after pulse to his cock. His cock swells in her mouth and she tries for more of the shaft as Santiago obsesses even more over her pussy. Santiago holds on to her thighs and helps her down onto his dick for a bit before pulling her back up so that his tongue is inside her again. They shoot into each other's mouths in a series of spasms and subdued breaths, followed by almost juvenile giggles. Now they're ready to fuck.

Facing each other now they kiss. The soft hair on Santiago's face turns Zarita on immensely. Her breasts rubbing against his chest does the same to him. Zarita parts her legs as Santiago's dick dances between her thighs, searching for the entrance to her love nest. She reaches for the condoms on the side table and places them in his hand. Sitting on his waist, just above the pulsating tip of his cock, she gives him the room he requires to get his condom on. The sound of the plastic rolling down his tool and then being stretched wide and released in a series of snaps at the base of his eleven inches confirms for Zarita that it's time.

She slides down onto the shaft and it fills her completely. This is not the position she wants to be in, needing to feel the power of the beast inside her and also on top of her. But she knows that Santiago won't disappoint her so she doesn't deny him a bit of what he loves. He holds on to her breasts as she circles hard over his cock. She feeds her nipples into his mouth as she squeezes each of the muscles in her vagina individually and then hugs the tip of his meat for as long as Santiago can take it. When he can't breathe, when he can no longer think, he begs her to free him. She does, relaxing her pussy muscles in sequence and Santiago releases an almost whining sound as she resumes her intense circling of the dick inside her before it has a chance to process the release.

Because of the bend in Santiago's dick, it hits every part of Zarita's vagina. So even though she needs an aggressive fuck tonight, she knows this round won't be it. She knows this because she can already feel that she is minutes from another orgasm. There's no turning back for her now, Santiago himself is still a good way away from his next one. Zarita holds onto Santiago tightly and squeezes. He grabs the sheets and also grips the side of the bed as he braces himself for an aggressive fucking from the woman on top of him. Zarita fucks him with the pace and power he knows she expects from him in a minute. She also fucks him with the knowledge that only she will have an orgasm this time around. So her work is a selfish endeavor for the most part.

With her pussy satiated and satisfied, Santiago eases her off of him and lays her on her stomach. She smiles, knowing what is about to happen. On her stomach, Santiago can see her swollen pussy, still dripping. But this isn't where he is going to be. He pulls her ass cheeks apart again and her tight hole yawns in anticipation. As it does, Santiago's finger finds the inside of her. He widens the hole by adding a second finger and then starts to move them around in wide circles, stretching the tight, tiny space. With his own dick now aching for a happy ending, he aligns his body with her, his tool positioned over her asshole, and with no real lubrication, he pushes down hard so that his cock is inside her in a single thrust.

He sends his arms under hers and then rests his hands on her head. Santiago essentially nails Zarita to the bed. She resists him, trying to get out from underneath him but not. She loves the game they play. He tightens his hold on her and keeps her locked in place. After letting her try to get away from him for a little while longer, and finally realizing that he isn't going to let her go anywhere, she relaxes into the bed and resigns herself very willingly to Santiago's bent cock ramming the shit out of her.

Santiago fucks her so that there is no doubt that she is being fucked. He searches every corner of her hole with the head of his torpedo and, finding it, slams into it hard. No part of her asshole isn't touched as he wraps his legs around hers and locks her further into him. He pushes down on her with every part of him and every inch of the surface of her skin makes constant contact with every part of him. Because his dick moves so aggressively inside her the feel of his curls against her make for an almost pleasant contrast. But this contrast is experienced in short bouts as his muscles make continuous contact with her almost as swiftly and the sensation morphs to a more intense one. The variations of sensations drive her insane and she moans loudly into the sheets.

Zarita loosens her grip on the bed and works for her hands under herself so that her fingers are on her relaxed cunt. She finds a beating hysterical mess there that opens up easily to her. She enters her pussy with her middle and index finger together and uses her other hand to push against the one inside her. She now fingers herself in response and mock opposition to what Santiago is doing to her. He knows to leave her, but not too long. He listens for the pace of her breathing and waits for his moment. Careful not to lose any of the intensity he is driving into her ass he listens still, monitoring her breathing and watching her elbows on either side of her, these being the only indication of the rapidness with which she is ripping into her cunt.

Just as her breathing becomes deep moaning Santiago removes one hand from Zarita's head and slips its arm from under hers. Holding her down with just one hand now, he uses the other to pull her arm from under her, and therefore her fingers from inside her. She almost bursts into a loud *fuck you* at the interruption to her pussy, already in climatic mode, but is immediately shut up by three thick fingers in her cunt that work to bring her to an explosive orgasm. She shakes violently underneath Santiago as he brings her to wave after orgasmic wave before he too starts to jerk uncontrollably on top of her, his own orgasm arriving almost on cue. He keeps his cock inside her for the time it takes both of them to recover from the shaking and to stabilize themselves on the bed. This was for both of them just what the doctor ordered.

They chat a little bit more about work while sitting in the bath in Zarita's en-suite. Santiago obsesses over the bastards that keep taking hard-earned cash from the business just because of their ethnic origins. He mulls various plans over in his head and keeps throwing ideas at Zarita, who tries to distract him with a hand job. He closes his eyes but doesn't stop talking even as he gets a full-on erection now and moves towards an unexpected orgasm. He cums under the water and then kisses Zarita, gratefully. She gets out first and hands him a towel, assuring him that everything is going to be okay.

Dressed again, Santiago goes downstairs while Zarita checks in on her daughter. Santiago pours them both coffee and hands Zarita her cup when she finally appears. The time that he took to make the coffee was just the time required for an idea to make an appearance as well. He knows just how to get this whole mess under control. There is just one person that needs to buy in to the plan. Zarita squints as he begins to lay out the plan. She giggles often as Santiago keeps a straight face while telling her that her body is going to be her saving grace. She is the sacrifice that will have to be made for her business's survival.

By the time they've finished their coffee, they know just how they'll be dealing with Preston Brink, the biggest prick at the head of all the bribery and extortion. They jot down what they know about Preston, which isn't much. But then they make a brief internet search and find out that Santiago's plan will definitely work because of the dynamics of Brink's family. It's an intriguing search and both Santiago and Zarita are delighted. Santiago outlines his plan again to his beautiful friend and notices how she is less resistant than she was a moment earlier. This is how they are going to take back their power.

CHAPTER 9

FOR THE NEXT WEEK, things in the office are pretty quiet. There is plenty of time for Santiago and Zarita to perfect their plan. So by the time she gets a call from Preston Brink that she should make sure that there's a little something for him in the office when he comes around later this morning, the pair are ready to set their plan into motion. Zarita checks herself in the bathroom, her hair in a very loose bun, and her white frock hanging delicately on her so that she looks like she should be naked. She looks out over her office floor at all the agents busy on the phones and knows that the presence of Brink always puts them on edge. This plan needs to work because these people don't deserve the stress placed on them by threats and lies.

For some reason known only to bullies like Hitler and Saddam, Preston feels the need to throw his weight around each time he comes to shake Zarita down. He raises his voice at anyone he comes into contact with, demanding to see the boss. He throws unfounded accusations of forged paperwork and couples these with threats of having the entire staff on the first plane back to Mexico. Everyone knows that this is possible, despite the fact that all of them are in the country legally. There are many stories doing the rounds of other Latinos who've not given in to being bribed and manipulated, and who all ended up being shut down and deported. So while there was no foundation for his threats, he was obviously able to fabricate the *foundation* he needed.

Preston Brink is an ambitious, overreaching thirty-year-old redneck. The weekend barbeques and nightly six-pack are evidenced by his gut. He is fat, but not excessively thanks to his generous height. He's almost seven feet to the inch. He's always impeccably dressed but his tie never sits snug on the collar. He needs the breathing space allowed by a loose top button and the tie hanging just above the second one. As Zarita runs out to meet him, asking him under her breath to please take it to her office, he takes her by the arm and leads her to the corner pocket that is hers as though he and not she was the boss around here. He gives the space his usual look around as though something new might pop out at him, and when nothing does, he shuts the door and sits in her chair.

He goes through the papers on her desk as if something in the writing will give him *real* leverage. He gets increasingly worked up as he realizes just how irreproachable this business actually is. The only thing that he actually has in his armor is the inherent insecurities of minority groups when faced with authority. And this is what Preston wants to be known as, *authority*. He loves the power that his position offers him, as a senior inspector at the local immigration center. It's up to him to ensure that immigrants aren't taking opportunities from deserving Americans. But when, as in cases like Zarita, there is nothing shady to capitalize on, he needs to make things up so that he can walk away with a fatter paycheck than he deserves. The cashback benefit from his manipulative streak means that he can keep the wife at home, a woman way above his station, happy and gifted with diamonds.

Zarita checks the door and locks it. She stands against it and watches the giant behind her desk. He drops her in-tray to the floor and then fiddles with her computer. She watches him go through her drawers and then check her purse. The look on his face lets her know that what he is looking for is not here. His expectations are definitely not being met. He gives Zarita a stern look and then questions her with his eyes and both hands in the air to either side of him.

"I just can't afford this anymore, Mr. Brink." Zarita clasps her hands together and looks at the floor.

"That's not a very good thing for you to be saying to me right now Miss Ordonez." He throws the contents of her purse to the floor.

Zarita runs to the side of her desk where Preston sits and starts to pick up her stuff. She takes deep breaths and transforms her anxious exhalations into very sexy sighs. She throws an exaggerated tantrum, mumbling in Spanish under her breath, moving in short swift moves that see her hair fall on her face, making her look vulnerable and sexy all at once. With her purse repacked she heaves a heavy sigh again before looking up at Brink, a *lost without options* look on her face. She watches his eyes and waits. She waits some more, still watching. And then she sees it, the glint in his eyes that signals the light-bulb moment where the alternative *in-kind* payment method registers.

On her knees, Preston sees down her dress, her perfect breasts almost jumping out at him. He clearly wonders why he hadn't thought of this before. But of course, being the largely inadequate last choice husband of the youngest daughter of the state governor, his priorities were clear. The job that his father-in-law had handed him paid him enough to make them comfortable, but not enough for him to treat his wife so that she could keep giving daddy a great report about him. But now, an opportunity for him to be in charge, to be powerful, to be in control, presents itself and is just too damn good to pass up. Zarita is fucking attractive, more so than his wife whose father was the real reason Brink was interested, and so what she is clearly offering him today is just what his ego, and his cock needs.

Preston is suddenly excited, talking to himself. He goes to the door and checks it twice to see if it's locked. He pulls the blinds despite them being on the third floor. Despite this though, the space is still very light and bright. He takes off his tie completely and releases the buttons all the way down his shirt. His belly flops out over his belt and he immediately undoes it, pulling down his zip too. His pants drop to the floor, leaving him in white boxers that seem too large even for him. He goes to where Zarita is still on the floor and takes her by her shoulders, bringing her to her feet. Suddenly the difference in size is obvious. His large frame excites her, but she doesn't let it show.

"I suppose we can play for a bit today. That will be alright. I mean, you gotta pay for your favors right. And if you ain't got cash for my favor, then it's only right that you do me a little favor right? You're an open-minded girl, right? I can tell you're open-minded…" Preston speaks like he's about to get something he always wanted but never thought he would ever have. He is completely enthralled by the opportunity that has presented itself.

"Yes, Mr. Brink, whatever you want sir, whatever you say," Zarita plays vulnerable *very* well.

Preston is now a very enthusiastic puppy. He keeps asking for her permission to touch her, permission she gives only with her eyes. He gives her a pleading look and whispers into her ear. She doesn't respond to him but he ties her hands behind her back with his tie so at some point her eyes again gave him the affirmative. With her hands tied Brink runs his fingers through her thick black hair and then bends to kiss her cheeks. He licks her neck repeatedly and then sticks his tongue into her ear. He helps her back down to her knees, his cock pitching a mean tent in his boxers.

Pulling his shorts to his knees he reveals a thick, fat, stump of a dick. It's not small, about eight inches, but it seems disproportionate to his frame. He points it down to Zarita and encourages her to open her mouth. She does, but he's too tall for her to reach his dick despite her best efforts. He gets onto his knees as well and his meat finally finds the inside of her mouth. His cock is juicy and tastes every bit like a good dick should. But his foreskin is thick and excessive and Zarita finds herself wishing that the bastard was circumcised. But he isn't and she just needs to do what she can about enjoying it.

The fuller his erection though the nicer he is to suck. And once he starts to ooze precum his dick head slides through the cover. With his head exposed Zarita gives his cock a very good suck. She fucks the living daylights out of his meat with just her mouth and both hands bound. Brink cannot believe it. His disbelief is clear on his face. He moves her occasionally off of his dick and holds her up so that she is able to lick his balls. He likes his balls wet. Then he has her on his cock again, sucking hard as he throws every profanity at her that comes to mind. She's turned on, and so is he. This couldn't be going any better if she had scripted it.

The combination of dick in her mouth and her hands

tied behind her wets her so much that the smell of her pussy filters up to Brink's nose. This scent is what every man wants to get because it confirms for him that he has managed to turn the woman he's going to fuck, on. This smell is one that Preston hasn't smelled in a very long time, his wife not the most sexually enlightened being he's ever known. But she loves him and so their sex life has been boring but acceptable. Zarita on the other hand has just driven his cock crazy and he begs her to bite into the meat of his shaft in addition to her awesome sucking. She bites into his meat hard and he again sends streams of precum into her mouth.

With his cock practically spewing its contents now, he pulls it from her mouth and lifts her to her feet. He turns her over and bends her over the desk. Brink is completely taken by the firmness of her ass. His hands move over her cheeks and squeeze them appreciatively. The knot on her wrists comes undone easily and her hands place firmly on the edge of her desk. She rests her head on the files on her table and turns so that her eyes face the cupboard on the wall to her right. There is a moment where Brink feels for her hole with a thick finger and moans loudly when he finds it.

"Wow, now that's tight. Gonna be a real squeeze." He stutters almost, under his breath.

Zarita is clever about her expression and looks every bit like a doe caught in the headlights. She knows that his dick is going to satisfy her in her favorite place to get fucked but she needs to be sure not to let the pleasure show. When Preston finds her hole with his dick he is very loud about his satisfaction with himself. Zarita lets out a subdued scream, not an act, but in a natural response to the fatness in her space. He fucks her like a man on the clock, and shoots his load into her in less than five.

Preston checks her ass for tell-tale signs of fucking, as if he doesn't want to leave any evidence of himself there. He pulls up her panties and pulls her dress back down to cover her. He dresses while she watches the sky through the slits in the blinds. Only once he is fully clothed does he clear his throat and Zarita turns around.

"That's some nice ass you have there Ordonez. But it won't keep my wife happy. So the next time I visit, you'd better have me some hard cash. You'd better have me some money you hear me, or you'll be having your tight ass fucked by a string of jalapenos all the way to Guatemala." The old Preston is back!

As soon as he has stepped out of her office Zarita raises the blinds and opens a window. The air cools the sweat on her breasts as she restores her bun. She gets her desk back in order and then sits on her chair so as to remind herself that she is the boss. She watches the cupboard for a while and squints at nothing. Her head goes to the side as she wonders why there is still no movement, ten minutes after it's just her in the office. Finally, the door rattles, and then the catch clicks undone, and out steps a red-faced, camera-wielding Santiago.

"I'm sorry, I was enjoying watching you!" They both laugh as he hands over the camera. He sports a massive hard-on as well and undoes his pants while Zarita checks the tape. Satisfied with the recording she takes Santiago into her mouth even though they both know that the door isn't locked. She pulls a massive load from him and swallows every last drop.

Santiago places the camera and its tapes in a designated safe place. Then they look up the contact details of Mr.

Brink and after a few phone calls they have the information they need to get in touch with Mrs. Brink and her father, the Californian governor of the state, should they ever need to. But the information itself, coupled with the contents of the recording will be enough to shut up the pig and get him and his cronies off of Zarita's back once and for all. She stares at Santiago as he puts his cock away, licks his lips, and smirks, "for a fat bastard, he wasn't half bad." They both laugh and order lunch.

CHAPTER 10

THE NEW SENSE of power and control that Zarita feels inspires her. With the extra money that she will now have in her pocket, she decides to set up new offices in Venice beach, so that they have access to higher quality clientele from the walk-in traffic on Venice. But the property prices are exorbitant, even with the extra dollars; she decides to take her time shopping around. Eventually, the perfect space presents itself and she arranges a viewing with the owner. She arrives at exactly nine AM and finds the entrance to the *vintage* whitewashed split-level loft walk-up already open. She lets herself in.

Jeff Davidson is almost sixty-five years old and looks it; But not in a bad way. He is the *never-worked-a-day-in-my-life-old-money-spend-everyday-in-the-gym-and-only-go-to-appointments-with-women-I-might-fuck* kind of sixty-five. He wears his Greek mother's heritage on his thick head of hair and on his face, his eyebrows think, his lashes long, and his lips full and perfect. He wears a soft salmon golf shirt and golf shorts. His loafers are Gucci. When he turns his head to meet her eyes, he is as surprised by her attractive-ness as she is by his.

They discuss the mathematics of the rental and the option that exists to buy. That she could be a property owner, especially of such prime real estate, excites her visi-bly. Jeff has been in the game long enough to know what this is the time to make himself the hero, the knight that has what she wants and can give it to her, provided she worked with him. Zarita is not naïve and understands from his tone and body language that the difference between the asking price for the property, and the new negotiated price, is *tucked between her thighs*. In light of her recent operation with Brink, this isn't an altogether undesirable option. But she can't decide without speaking to Santiago first.

"Is he a grease ball?" Santiago asks, obviously needing to make a comparison with himself.

"He would be an easier fuck than Brink, and more beneficial." She speaks of it like a transaction, with abso-lutely no awkwardness since the person she speaks to is the very man who opened her up to the possibilities that existed inside her vagina.

"And what if he just keeps wanting more and more even after you've paid for the place?" The sensibility is almost stern.

"He can't, not if I buy it outright, at the new price on the table."

"The price that includes your pussy on the table, not just once I would imagine. You know he won't let that much money go for one dip in your quesadilla." There's a tinge of bitterness in his reference to her pussy.

"We could make it a once-off, maybe with a recording of sorts, like with Brink. Davidson is on several boards and his grandson was just accepted into a prestigious rowing program in Europe. Any scandal would be most unwelcomed."

"That means that the fucking would have to be scandalous, how would you do that?" Santiago wants to know.

"Leave that up to me. You feel much like playing cameraman?" She throws him a naughty smile.

He returns her smile with a *'there's suddenly too much traffic in your pussy for my liking'* look, turns the lights off in the entire floor using the master panel on the inside of Zarita's office, and then fumbles towards her in the dark as his eyes adjust to the slivers of light streaming through the slits in the blinds. He gets to the desk just as she comes into view, pulls her to her feet, and sends his hand under her skirt. He pushes through her panties and sends the soft lace along with the tip of his finger into her pussy. His lips fall on hers as her mouth becomes a smile and then he finds the inside of her mouth with his tongue. If Santiago is going to watch her get fucked by someone else again, he is going to make sure that he is as sexually satisfied as possible before he does, the pain of an unattended erection unbearable, even with a post-recording blowjob.

"You're a very attractive woman Zarita. There is absolutely no reason why you shouldn't be able to use it to get what you want. It's better than having it exploited by dogs that just use you for what they want."

"Is that a yes then Santiago, will you shoot the little video of Mr. Davidson and my attractive self?" She just needs him to say yes.

"Yes, of course, I will. We just need to set it up. But for now..." He finishes the sentence by pulling her panties down a little and sending his finger into her completely.

There is fire exchanged between them as their tongues collide. They remain locked while Zarita manages to get Santiago's cock out through the zipper of his pants. He walks her to the wall without removing his finger from her pussy. Once he has her against the wall he adds another finger and double-digits her cunt for a minute. She soon lifts her skirt and begs him to fuck her, whereupon he lowers himself a little on his haunches and directs his dick into her aching pussy. No sooner has he started to thrust and the ache makes a slow and graceful exit.

Santiago fucks her for four hours without speaking. His head is consumed with the idea of another man inside her, an idea that he had opened her up to and so had no right now to question. He hits every part of her pussy, as usual, taking extra care today to send his bend into her g-spot over and over again. She makes no attempt to muffle the sound of her pleasure, her pussy completely relaxed in the knowledge that her little Nina was in the care and keeping of her babysitter. Santiago morphs between fucking Zarita and making love to her, and she has no idea which it is that brings her to her climax. But whichever one it is, it has not milked Santiago's dick yet, a side-effect of his obsessed focus on pleasing her.

He turns her around so that her breasts are against the wall and her ass perked and raised in the direction of his dick. He eases his cock into her butt with help from Zarita herself. She pushes her tight hole onto him, especially since there is not a drop of moisture on his cock, or on her tight asshole. The squeeze is incredibly intense tonight, probably because Santiago's cock has an added girth of two inches. This is one of the strange phenomena of his cock. It never extends to its full length or expands to its full girth on a regular day. But if he fucks for an extended period, or if his fucking is particularly charged, say by emotion, than this massive augmentation makes an appearance. It is front and center tonight.

The condom seems to be keeping Santiago from cumming, and so he exits her hole and asks permission to disrobe his warrior. He frees his cock and then gives her generous ass a good licking. He makes certain to pour as much saliva onto the hole as he can and then gets back to his feet. His cock slides into her hole surprisingly smoothly, Zarita opening up to the almost eight-inch girth with ease. His cock starts to beat deep within itself and Santiago feels a tingle in his nuts that lets him know that if he doesn't shoot a load soon he's going to be in a lot of pain by morning. He pulls her away from the wall slightly and bends her forward. Zarita holds on to the wall and takes every piercing stroke of Santiago's mamba for the ten minutes he takes to fill the inside of her ass with what feels like liters of hot wax.

The appointment with Jeff is set up for two days later. It has to be in Zarita's office because of the convenience of the cupboard they've already custom-modified for Santiago and his camera. The appointment is an after-hours arrangement, and Jeff arrives promptly at seven. The floor is dark for the most part, and Zarita has music playing in her office so that should Santiago move unexpectedly in the cupboard, it could be explained away by the soft rock coming from the speakers in the ceiling. Santiago settles into the cupboard with seconds to spare, Jeff's soft knock on the door opening it, to his and Zarita's surprise.

"This isn't a bad space you have here Miss Ordonez." Jeff admires the building for both its location and its architecture. It's an arrogant admiration of the building he'd owned for almost two decades before selling it to Zarita's current and soon-to-be-ex landlord.

"Yes, it is. But it isn't Venice Beach." Zarita makes it clear what she wants.

"So how badly do you want to be in Venice Beach?" He asks this as he fiddles with the light switches until just the downlights cast an amber glow on everything in the room. He loves what this light does to the color of her skin and confirms with a wink that he's set the perfect ambiance.

"I suppose I want to be in Venice Beach almost as badly as you want to be *in me*, Mr. Davidson." She knows to let him take the lead from now on if the taping is going to be of any use to her. She can't appear to have seduced him or bribed him with her cunt. It would be too easy for his wife to forgive.

The contract is placed on the table, and a sale offer with almost four hundred thousand dollars knocked off the asking price. She looks at the figures, and at the clauses. Nothing in it mentions her pussy.

"Make me happy little miss, and we can sign off on this right here, tonight!" He's just hit a nail in his own coffin.

"What do you mean sir?" She needs him to repeat it just so she can be sure they get it on tape.

"Come now Zarita, you want what I've got and I'm prepared to give it to you. With a pretty thing like you, things could get very uncomfortable very quickly. But play nice with me and you'll own my building by morning." He has just made the tape a thousand times more potent than just fucking would have done. Zarita is clever not to say anything else, simply looking down at the ground and playing the confused minority being offered her dreams by a sex-crazy pervert.

Jeff is an aggressive lover, much to Zarita's delight. He lifts her off the chair and then pulls her dress off her shoulders. He reaches behind her and unfastens her bra, dropping it to the floor. He takes her nipples between his fingertips and squeezes hard. Jeff takes them into his mouth in turn and sucks on her breasts while rubbing his cock. He instructs Zarita to put her hands on him and to make his cock hard. He needs her to bring about the effect of the pills he swallowed an hour before he arrived here. She obliges him, giving his crotch a good squeeze and then rubbing her hand over the area where his cock should be. She is met by massive balls instead.

"Keep going baby, give it a good squeeze, wake up the old boy. Come on, you can do it. Squeeze harder..." Jeff tries not to frustrate himself at the risk of nullifying the Viagra. He sucks on her nipples again, sucks on her neck, and then back onto her breasts. As his cock starts to warm up he plants a grateful kiss on her lips. His thick tongue slides into her mouth as well and the heat of this connection makes her wish he was licking her pussy.

Jeff gets his belt loose and his pants off just as his erection fills his underwear. He pulls his underwear off to just under his nuts and reveals a decent-sized cock. The tool is firm and ready for action. He gets the belt was undone that keeps Zarita's dress on her waist. The floral mess falls to the ground, followed quickly by her panties. Jeff wets his finger in her mouth and then feeds it to her cunt. He pays careful attention to the tightness of the squeeze. When this finger moves easily in and out of her he adds another. He moves the two around inside her until they too move around easily. A third addition fills her cunt and he is more aggressive about making the three fit. They eventually also move around easily inside her now dripping cunt.

He pushes her to her knees and hits his cock against her forehead a few times before putting it into her mouth. The sound of it against her head makes her want to giggle.

Santiago almost rolls out of the cupboard in his efforts to contain his own laughing. Once Jeff has his meat in her mouth he fucks her hard between her pretty lips, admiring the sight of his hard cock sliding in and out of her, very vocal about the heat he finds there. He lets slip that this might be the best discount he's given yet. Again Zarita hides her pleasure at Jeff Davidson's loose mouth. He's really added some killer dialogue to her little piece of blackmail.

She can't help but reward him for falling so hard into her trap. With her mouth still on his dick, she runs her tongue around the head while sucking on it at the same time. Her mouth takes Jeff on a trip he has never been on before, but looking at her lips, wrapped over his thick shaft and not giving any evidence of what is going on behind the red, you would never guess it. Between her legs, Zarita contracts and relaxes the muscles of her vagina, so that she can control the resistance when Jeff needs to get his medication-supported boner inside her. As he starts to fuck her mouth more vigilantly, her cunt becomes more and more excited at the idea of having the same action delivered to it. So, without waiting for him, she moves her mouth off his dick and stands up.

"We're not done yet Miz, not by a long shot. Where do you think you're going?" Jeff asks as Zarita paces for a minute in front of him and then walks to her desk directly under the lights so that she starts to *shimmer*. She throws her arms around herself as though she was getting cold, covering her breasts, but leaving her vagina visible. This has the desired effect because now Jeff's focus is her cunt.

He smiles at her and pulls the paperwork to him. He reaches for a pen and gives Zarita several winks before signing his property over to her, on condition of course that she can secure the finance for it in thirty days. This is a no-brainer for Ordonez who has a very healthy relationship with her bank. And so, with the details are out of the way, she finalizes her security tape, the collateral that will mean there are no comebacks from this man who has now shot his dick into her with the virility of a twenty-year-old. He hits her hard for a good two hours, running his mouth in every direction until he finally pulls his cock from her, pushes her to her knees, and jerks off onto her face. His load isn't excessive and he uses his fingers to direct his cum from her cheeks to her mouth. She licks his fingers at his direction.

By the time Jeff has left the building Santiago is almost block-stiff in the cupboard. He should really have considered a career in espionage. Zarita helps him from the cupboard and then pries the camera from his fingers before she gives him a much-needed massage. They give the visit from Davidson a watch, and once they're satisfied, Santiago drives Zarita home in her car where she has a shower while he soaks in the bath. They fuck passionately before leaving each other to the dreams and excitement that comes from having a new office.

They move in to the new space, and just as expected, business is good...Very Good!

CHAPTER 11

IN THE THIRD month in the new space, everyone is making money. Zarita has a relaxed aura about herself that has everyone gravitate naturally toward her. The decor of the space is an authentic reflection of how great she feels and how good life is going. Santiago is her bona fide right hand now, second in command to her alone. The staff contingent has grown to an eclectic mix of Latinos and a few other minorities, with just the girl manning reception an *all American*. The lot of them gels well and this makes itself known in the figures. *Everyone* is happy.

When Jeff arrives unannounced Zarita is surprised to say the least. She had forgotten about the tape for the most part and hopes that this isn't an indication that she might need to bring it into play. He has his money, all of it. She has a mortgage. For a minute as she watches him in the visitor's chair in her office and tries to remember if the sex was good enough to be worth a repeat. She tries her imagination for something, anything that might make her want to be fucked by Jeff again. It has to be for fun, it has to benefit her.

She won't be doing it just for the sake of it. Her cunt isn't needy, Santiago taking very good care of her.

Jeff doesn't sit this time, pacing in the front of her desk instead. She knows what he wants and so she opens her computer and accesses her email.

"I hope you don't mind Jeff, I just need to get this email gone, and then *I'm all yours*." She lets the end of the sentence trail off in a hive of suggestion and Jeff receives the suggestion with a smile. For the next three minutes, she exchanges a series of emails with Santiago while Jeff stares at her in anticipation. She needs to get his take on what she sees now as an opportunity, but an opportunity for what? They own the property. They don't need another. So what could fucking Jeff, right now, benefit Zarita and her business? She needs Santiago's advice, as usual.

Keep him wanting! This is the final instruction from Santiago who is across town for meetings and so is emailing from his Blackberry. Zarita knows that this means that he will probably have a plan by sundown but for now she just needs to be sure not to alienate Mr. Davidson.

Jeff and Zarita speak in whispers about fucking, as if there are ears in the walls. It's cute to watch such a powerful man beg silently for her pussy is a turn-on. Zarita hadn't realized until just now that she held the secrets to every man's weakness between her thighs. Life didn't have to be *inconvenient* ever again. And all she had to do was make sure that Jeff Davidson's cock burned for her, at least until she gets what she wants from him. She just needs to wait for Santiago to tell her *what* she wants.

She locks the door herself this time. Jeff panics and lets her know that he will need some *help*. She knows what he means and assures him that if he just relaxes, she can get the desired results all around. "You really don't need to get hard for the nerves in your cock to work," she whispers as she unzips him and pulls out his soft cock. She gets it into her mouth and gives it a slow, gentle suck. She puts no pressure on the cock, trying for absolutely nothing except enjoying the taste and feel of it in her mouth. Jeff is completely surprised by the sensations moving through him in the absence of an erection. She is in absolutely no rush as she sucks on Jeff for as long as it takes for him to shake slightly, exhale hard, and cum in her mouth. He shoots one of the biggest loads he has in a while and he lets Zarita know this. She smiles and sends him on his merry way.

When Santiago meets her at the office after the last of the staff has left, he has enough information to get them a massive payday. Jeff Davidson plays golf with not just the governor, but also with their old friend, and the governor's son-in-law, *Preston*. Jeff and Preston are as upstanding as the governor, from the outside. But Santiago and Zarita know better. They also know now that falling out of favor with the governor will be the worst thing that could happen to the pair. The governor's conservative manner would never stomach the contents of the videos. And if they can add one more super-sleazy performance, then it will be Zarita blackmailing Preston, and it will be Zarita's company that will be handling the insurance requirements of all of Jeff's properties. ***They decide on a final video***!

The first step is to set up the office for the shoot. A downtown contact with a surveillance background installs the cameras in Zarita's office. They check them against the amber lighting that Jeff liked, and the result is amazing. The cameras will run nonstop for the next seven days and feed to a remote recording station set up in Santiago's apartment. The easiest part of their highly devious, deliciously erotic plan has been taken care of. The next step is going to require perfect timing and perfect placement. Santiago again is the captain of the ship.

It's not too hard for them to locate Preston, and with the passing of a few hundred dollars, Santiago and his surveillance buddy are seated right behind Brink and some of his mates at the local country club. Once they are sure that they are being listened to, they speak about the sex-crazy Ordonez who keeps begging to be double-banged. They layout imaginary events where the two of them have repeatedly fucked the hot tiny pussy in the new office that has her feeling like the queen of Venice Beach. Santiago knows that Preston knows him by sight and so the entire story registers with Brink as believable. They can only hope that he takes the bait and plays it the way they imagine. By night time they know it's worked, *wonders!*

Jeff sends her a text around six. Zarita is alone in the office as usual, but this time it's because she has received several texts from Preston all day demanding to see her. She responds to him just after six, when she responds to Jeff. They'll both be getting here around seven. Zarita knows that they'll probably have discussed her by the time they get here, so she works herself up so that she is ready for them when they arrive. She taps her clit repeatedly so that her pussy is warm and moist by the time she buzzes her visitor up. Preston has arrived first. He hasn't even sat down when she buzzes Jeff in. The two men look at each other and make a transparent attempt at pretending not to know each other. There is no sound on the video feed and so the content of their conversation is really irrelevant.

"I'm a busy woman, gentlemen. You've both been hitting up my phone over the last while wanting a minute of my time. *This* is your minute." She looks the odd pair up and down, one is a healthy sixty-five with a nice cock, and the other is a younger giant with a nice cock. So at least she gets a double dose of nice cock. They look at each other with a little more than familiarity now. They look at each other with the hint of strategy, before they proceed. Santiago settles into the comfort of his leather lazy-boy in his lounge where he watches the events play out on the tiny screen in front of him, his hand in his track-pants and his fingers plying his penis.

Jeff moves in first and stands in front of a seated Zarita. Without thinking he rubs Zarita's lips against his cock over his beige chinos. This isn't a very good idea, his crotch streaked with lipstick. He'll figure it out later, and unzips his pants, pulls his cock through, and encourages it into Zarita's mouth. He obviously enjoyed the soft suck she gave him the last time she sucked his cock. This time though, he's had his helpers already and his dick hardens fast in her mouth. Preston moves in, armed with a necktie he's been carrying in his pocket. Zarita knows what to expect.

Preston manages to tie her hands behind her back while she stays seated, and then pulls up so that the tie then loops around her neck. She has her arms crossed high up near the middle of her back this time, Preston remembering how he couldn't access her ass the last time without untying her. He bites into the back of her neck while Jeff keeps fucking her mouth. The sight of it all hardens Preston and he removes his clothes completely. Jeff removes his shirt and then undoes his buckle so that his pants are now gathered around his ankles. He has no briefs on.

With his cock dripping now, Preston asks his co-star for a gap. He obliges, and Preston sends his dick into Zarita's mouth. His fleshy foreskin again is a bit of an issue for her but Preston seems to realize this and he pulls back his skin while she fucks her mouth. He does manage to get his dome head clear of the excess skin and Zarita rewards him with the skill of her tongue. Preston quickly starts his dripping and Zarita's mouth is given generous doses of precum. He brings himself close again without intending to and pulls his penis out of her mouth. He lifts her to her feet.

Preston moves her between them, him at the back with a hand on the part of the tie stretching between her neck and arms. He wants to be in her ass. He needs to be in her ass. Brink bends a bit and parts her cheeks with his hands. He pushes her forward a bit and Jeff goes down on his haunches a bit so that he can kiss her while cupping her breasts. He pulls hard on her tits while sucking her tongue into his mouth hard. Preston gets all the way onto his needs, and after licking her ass repeatedly takes a few deep breaths around her cunt, needing the confirmation of his effect on her that is offered him by the smell of her pussy. He parts her legs and fingers her cunt hard while asking her for oral confirmation that she loves it.

Zarita pulls her mouth from Jeff's to answer Preston. Her affirmative has Jeff throw his eyes to her cunt, where Preston is digging into it with four fat fingers. He adds two of his own and repeats the request for oral confirmation of pleasure. They finger her hard with multiple digits and soon are both on their knees so that they can see exactly what they are doing. Zarita rains onto their hands and both of their cocks suddenly ache to be inside her. Preston pulls her cunt juice and drags it to her ass, sending his fingers into this space, coating it with her own juices. He stands up, leading Jeff to his feet too, and while he sends his dick into Zarita's ass, Jeff plows into cunt with his impressively firm cock.

They fuck her standing, albeit uncomfortably. Preston is tall behind her and so with each one of his thrusts into her ass he either pushes her forward or lifts her off Jeff's cock completely. The frustration of having to constantly reinsert his cock irritates Jeff so that he convinces Preston to lean back against the table and then lift Zarita onto it. So both Preston and Zarita are now reclined somewhat, and Jeff can lean over Zarita and dig comfortably into her vagina. They fuck her like this until the edge of the table cuts a neat red line across Preston's lower back, just above his ass. The discomfort is finally enough to force him to give up her ass. He lifts her off his cock as Jeff moves back slowly, his cock still in her pussy when she is placed back on the floor. He keeps fucking her, hard, aggressive, while Preston gathers himself.

Jeff turns around so that *he* is now leaning against the edge of the table, Zarita half lying on top of him as he ravages her cunt. On his haunches from the back, Preston shoots into her ass a few times again. He dips his dick into her repeatedly and then guides his head to where Jeff's cock is getting some serious pussy pleasure. He takes firm hold of his dick and finds Jeff's rhythm, joining his mass to Jeff's and then entering Zarita's pussy as well. The two dicks split Zarita almost in half. She is so glad that the shrills of orgasmic pleasure escaping her are inaudible. She does hide her face in Jeff's chest just in case the pleasure is visible on her face. They double dig into her cunt until she has the most aggressive orgasm she can remember. The tag team continues to double tap her pussy until first Preston, and then Jeff shoots into her. All three of them are incapable of hiding their pleasure.

The two men push Zarita down and tell her to suck on their balls and lick their dicks of the river of warm custard fusing on them. She cleans the rods with her tongue and then takes both sacks into her mouth, sucking and licking the warm bags. They hit their cocks on her face and then push them into her mouth again, encouraging her to suck again even though the tools are now soft. They force both cocks into her mouth at the same time and she sucks on them so well that they both cum again before they leave her in a sexed-out sweaty heap on her office floor.

Santiago arrives within the hour to help her gather her exhausted self and get home. He tells her how great the performance was, *all around*, and lets her know that she would never have to sleep with them again, unless she actually *wanted* to. The tapes have everything they need to get *everything* that they want.

"They were fucking hot actually," She tells Santiago in Spanish. "I might give them one or two more goes." The smile on her face is a serious one.

Santiago isn't happy with her sense of humor and hardly speaks to her while they edit the tapes. As usual, he is turned on by watching the sexy Zarita being *handled*. He knows what her mouth can do and so when he sees Jeff's and the Preston's dicks in her mouth he needs to remove his dick from his pants. He is desperate for the same oral action but isn't sure if Zarita is up to it. She is in nothing but his gown, having had a much-needed bath before they got down to the editing. He is comfortable enough to stroke his cock in her presence, a compliment to her as he keeps commenting positively on her ability, and her appearance. But he really wants the same oral action.

Zarita giggles to herself at her buddy's frustration and then leans over to swallow his bend. She sucks on him with all the tender attention the long-suffering Santiago deserves. She sucks some more until he can feel what he knows drove the two men on the tape crazy. Zarita brings Santiago to three orgasms before she takes her mouth off his cock.

Santiago gets on his knees between her legs and parts the gown so that her damp cunt is his to have. He eats out her pussy with the attentiveness the hardworking cunt deserves. Zarita and Santiago then make love on the soft carpeting of the living room floor. They exit, shower, and then drive to Zarita's house where they play video games with Nina while eating takeout. They know exactly what they are going to do with their tapes. The only question now is when...

CHAPTER 12

THE POWER of sex in Los Angeles was now something that Zarita understood well. It wasn't something that was the domain solely of Hollywood. She's enjoyed the two Caucasian cocks that have developed what is now an obvious fascination with her vagina. She enjoys *them* as much as they do her. But with all the work that has been going into her business now, she is making enough money, as are all her people, for her to now only do what she enjoys. There is nothing that satisfies her more than good sex; nothing except making money of course. Securing the future of her daughter is her primary prerogative.

While wrapping up another late-night session, Santiago and Zarita discuss a final tryst with the two players who can add significantly to the bottom line of the business. Santiago is a man though before he is Zarita's buddy. And the man in him needs to play a game of mine-is-bigger-than-yours with Jeff and Preston. Between him and Zarita, they decide that they are going to get the two together again, for the last time, and they are going to let them know what they have, and what they want. They want Preston to bring Zarita the full scope of the insurance business that is to be found at the Immigration department. And Jeff has a property empire that needs constant insurance coverage. Zarita will give Jeff this service. But they will not make the revelation of the *spy tapes* a harsh one. They plan on giving the two an intense orgasmic farewell ride first. The difference this time will be first, that there will be no recording, and secondly, that *Santiago will be present.*

Santiago arrives at the office first on this rainy Sunday morning. It's a dark day with the entire surface of the west coast sky a dark grey. It's the perfect setting for a ménage and Santiago can't resist recording it. He hopes that the other men will be open to having him as an addition, and also that once he reveals the taping to Zarita later, she will derive as much enjoyment from it as he knows he will. He checks the hidden control panel and makes sure that the system is turned on and that it is recording. Zarita is surprised to find him already in her office.

She hands Santiago a cup of coffee and a package from the drugstore. He opens the brown bag and finds several packs of condoms and a tiny tube of strawberry-scented lube. They chat for a minute about the possibilities of the morning and Santiago makes notes in his head to outdo the two who have both just pulled up outside and texted Zarita to announce their arrival. They find the door unlocked and let themselves in. The large black glass buzzes loudly behind them, shutting and locking itself. They chat casually as they walk up the stairs to the third floor that is the private office of Zarita Ordonez.

"This is Santiago, an old fuck buddy of mine." She answers all the questions Jeff and Preston aren't asking in her simple introduction.

"I hope you don't mind the third man?" Santiago says casually as he shakes both their hands.

"Not at all," Jeff answers.

"No, not..." Preston confirms.

They are both obviously a little thrown by the addition though, but say nothing, knowing that the real reason for them being here hasn't changed, and there is enough of Zarita for everybody.

The atmosphere in the room is clearly all about Zarita. She makes sure that they all know that this particular session is all about her. She runs her hands over all three crotches, her fingers met by huge bulges already swollen under the trousers in the room. She squeezes Jeff's cock firmly and then runs her fingers across the length of the shaft. She pulls him down so that he kisses her as she gives his cock a good go with her hands while their tongues heat the room. She gets him rock hard before disengaging her lips from his. He smiles at this controlling *mamacita* that obviously has a plan for all of them.

Zarita gets onto her reinforced glass table, the surface clear, and undresses in a rhythm that has her appear like she is dancing in the air to music that plays only in her head. Santiago helps the moment by turning on the surround sound and feeding sexy souls into the speakers all around them. The three of them watch her remove all her clothes, underwear included, and then they take their own clothes off. They find chairs on which to place their expensive threads and then pull on their cocks as Zarita gets down on her knees and then onto her back, her legs bent at the knee and her feet firmly on the glass.

Jeff is the first on the table. He straddles her face and drops his balls into her mouth. She bites on them and then sucks the sack. Preston and Santiago are on either side of the table stroking her from her breasts, down her legs, all the way to her toes. Preston pulls his leg towards him, as does Santiago, Zarita's vagina gaping on the glass. The reflections are beautiful. Preston bends down and starts to eat her breasts. He bites harder than he has before, his excitement exaggerated. Her breasts are sucked so incredibly passionately that it surprises Zarita that it isn't Santiago sucking on them. Jeff's balls are now his cock in her mouth, her entire breast in Preston's mouth before her nipples are at the total mercy of his tongue. Santiago's finger finds the inside of her pussy at just the right moment, completing the circuit of her chemistry.

The three men work their respective stations with expert precision. Santiago handles the bulk of the pressure, dealing with both her ass and her cunt. Preston on her breasts is doing an amazing job. Jeff has the most prime position, his cock satisfying Zarita's love for sucking dick. The circuit stays sealed for a good hour before the three men agree to reposition the beauty, Jeff and Zarita the only two having orgasmed. Preston and Santiago get her onto all fours, still on the table, and Jeff joins them on the ground. Jeff has clearly got a fixation with Zarita's mouth, his lips on hers already as he stands in front of her. The other two don't seem to mind as they seem to have their own plans for her.

Zarita kisses Jeff back because he kisses very well. They enjoy each other's mouths while Santiago slides under her. The glass is cold on his ass and he giggles at how uncontrollably he shivers. Zarita has done nothing to warm the glass despite her ass being perfectly imprinted on it. Holding his cock up, Santiago settles Zarita's pussy onto it and feeds her his meat from below. Once the connection has been established with her vagina, she takes it upon herself to ride

Santiago like the stallion he is. After testing the table for sturdiness, Preston mounts Zarita himself. From above, her eases his dick into her ass and fucks her to the same rhythm with which she is fucking the man underneath her. Jeff's cock is in her mouth again.

Another hour passes and the group manages a superb simultaneous orgasm. Preston is the first to pull his cock from her, much to Zarita's disappointment. She really loves having her ass plugged. He makes his way to where Jeff is losing the battle now to maintain an erection. The older man gives the younger space, and Zarita's mouth fills with Preston's fat cock. She sends her tongue into his foreskin and dances around the head. It takes just three thrusts to expose his head. She does enjoy the taste of his meat.

Jeff is behind her now, eating out her ass. He sends his tongue deep into her ass and works it around inside the hole. She wants to scream and so she does. Every time she moves her ass away from Jeff's mouth when the pleasure becomes too much for her, she ends up squeezing onto Santiago's dick with her vagina. She fucks it for a good couple of thrusts before she raises her ass back into Jeff's mouth. Jeff's cock is now completely flaccid and so he uses his mouth and fingers to dig into Zarita's ass, not doing a half-bad job. He does such a good job in fact that she begs for a dick in her ass.

Santiago's dick is still rock solid inside her. Zarita is able to pivot on the tool so that she now sits perched on his dick but with her back to him and a disappointed Preston. She faces Jeff, who looks like he's suddenly got an idea. But before he can execute, Santiago lifts Zarita off of his dick and then holds her up as she feeds her asshole his cock. Once the length of it is inside her ass, she reclines so that her back relaxes on Santiago's chest and he is able to kiss the side of her face and her neck. With his hands on her hips, Santiago slides her up and down his dick, fulfilling every one of her ass's fantasies.

Preston lays across her face so that he forms a perfect right angle with Santiago's body. He positions himself as though he's about to do a set of pushups. This is exactly what he starts doing, and he fucks Zarita's mouth in this position, grateful that his arms are stronger than they appear. Zarita is also happy for this thick occupant in her mouth again. The fingers fiddling with her clitoris can only belong to Jeff. He seems to be working up to something but Zarita isn't sure what. He seems to be determined to stretch her cunt and loosen it at the same time, adding, at last, the strawberry-scented lube that has gone unnoticed all day. He lathers her cunt with it and then gives it a lick, pleased that it tastes like it smells.

Totally unexpected, Jeff feeds his flaccid cock into a very receptive Zarita. Her vagina is a hot, slippery mess and Jeff is the pig digging around inside it. The feeling of the soft cock inside her is strange, but the contrast between it and the hard dick in her ass and mouth make for another interesting circuit. With everyone having already had more than one orgasm, it takes almost two full hours of wild thrusting and deep concentration before all of them are again having an almost simultaneous orgasm. Their climax is a series of ripples that sees them fold like dominos into and onto one another. This has been the most intense fucking for all of them for as long as they can remember. They sit naked on the floor sipping on bottled water and champagne leftover from the massive opening months earlier.

Santiago and Zarita give each other a questioning look. They wonder about the tapes they want to reveal. But then

Zarita asks the two about the possibility of them sending some business her way. The answer surprises Santiago and herself, both of them enthusiastically offering up their networks and contacts. Both men even insist on getting her the governor's attention, his office able to send hundreds of thousands of dollars in annual revenue her way. Everyone agrees that this is an altogether pleasant arrangement, one that could become a regular thing, once or twice a month with no pressure until they're bored. The revelation of the tapes is suddenly not necessary, for now.

The progression from good to great is made with ease, and Zarita and her people soon own the Los Angeles insurance industry. Money is made all around and all the dreams she had for herself and her daughter slowly become a reality. Santiago Sanchez eventually, with the help and motivation of little Nina, asks Zarita out on a real date. It takes a couple of months for her to finally agree, not wanting to mess up what has for years now been a very good thing. They go out a couple of times, still fitting in the odd session with Jeff and Preston. Finally, the dating starts to feel like dating, and the possibility of exclusivity comes up. They're open-minded and adventurous enough to add to the party from time to time should they wish. This wishing doesn't happen, the bend in Santiago's dick becoming insanely possessive of the spicy Zarita Ordonez.

ABOUT THE AUTHOR

Heather Stolts

Heather Stolts is an emerging erotica author of many erotica kinks and sub-genres. Be sure to check out other books and leave a review if this story got you hot!

Visit my blog at Heather Stolts Blog

Join my newsletter for exclusive previews Heather Stolts Newsletter

Sign up for Free Stories from Xplicit Press Authors

Xplicit Press Author Updates

Like Xplicit Press on Facebook

Follow Xplicit Press on Twitter

Readers: I want to expand a few of the stories to see where the characters can be explored further. If there are any of the stories that you would like to read more about again, I'd love to hear from you!

Keep In Touch
Heather Stolts
info@heatherstolts.com